Easton Island
A Most Unusual Guest

Hope Callaghan

hopecallaghan.com

Visit my website for new releases and special offers: hopecallaghan.com

D1716000

CONTENTS

Cast of Characters

Morgan Easton. Morgan has been handed several heartbreaking blows, including the loss of her mother, Laura Locke Easton. A mysterious letter from an attorney arrives, inviting her to the reading of her mother's will in a place she's never heard of.

Morgan soon discovers family secrets that will change her life forever. Does she have the courage to claim what rightfully belongs to her and start over?

Quinn Schultz. Morgan's best friend who sticks by her side as she navigates her way through her new life on Easton Island.

Elizabeth Easton. The backbone of the Easton family dynasty, Elizabeth welcomes Morgan into the family with open arms. Wisely understanding it won't be easy and certain her granddaughter will face some resistance from the islanders, she sets the course for the continuation of Easton Island and Easton Holdings while staying close to Morgan, knowing some of the island's secrets will have her granddaughter reeling.

Brett Easton. Morgan's half-brother who runs Easton Holdings. Despite making an effort to include her in the family business, in the back of her mind, Morgan wonders if his willingness to include her is too good to be true.

Veronica "Ronni" Lansbury. Laura Easton's close friend, who proves to be a valuable ally, determined to help guide Morgan along the path she's certain Laura would have wanted.

Chapter 1

Morgan glanced at her watch for the umpteenth time, an inkling of nervousness settling in. The flight she and her grandmother were waiting on had been delayed for takeoff, with no indication about why it sat on the ground an hour past its scheduled departure. "I thought their plane would have already landed by now."

Grandmother Elizabeth patted her arm. "It will be all right. Randi may be a bit...eccentric, but I'm sure she won't be too difficult of a guest."

"I'm not worried about Randi's stay at Locke Pointe. It's the reason for her visit that has me stressed out."

Ever since Morgan and Wyatt had found the Shifting Sands Medallion, what was believed to be an ancient artifact the previous December, she'd gone back and forth from believing it was authentic to convincing herself there was no way she had a priceless piece of history in her possession.

Randi Colbane, a world-renowned Biblical archaeologist, would soon verify what Morgan had on her hands, which created a new set of problems. What to do with it if it was, in fact, authentic.

And to add another layer of stress, rumors had been swirling the last few weeks about Colbane being spotted in the area. Several local newspapers, including the island's Easton Harbor Beacon, had run stories about the medallion's history, most recently mentioning several "informed" sources placing the artifact on Easton Island.

"We shall finally have our answer and the answer will set you free," Elizabeth quipped.

"Or cause me more grief and headache than I'm ready for," Morgan muttered.

"There's always the option of not having the medallion authenticated. We could turn Randi right back around on the plane and leave it locked in Easton Estate's safe."

"As much as the idea sounds tempting, I can't. I would be letting my grandparents and mother down. I was meant to find it."

"I agree. I believe you were, which means we proceed with the plan. Authenticate, verify and then figure out our next step," the senior Easton said. "It is going to be a busy week, particularly for you."

Not only was Morgan entertaining her special visitor, but she was also running what had already become an increasingly popular bed-and-breakfast with a steady stream of guests arriving and departing.

Thank goodness for her staff, who worked hard to ensure each guest's visit was perfect. In fact, getting it up and running was going almost a little too smoothly.

"Between Greg Baker, Tina, my cook, my cleaning gals and Ronni helping with managing and the admin stuff, Locke Pointe is running like a well-oiled machine."

"I'm so proud of you. I knew you could do it and now you've proven to everyone, including Prissy Finkpin, that she was wrong." Elizabeth ran the tip of her finger over her chin, a mischievous twinkle in her eye. "Now that I think about it, perhaps it's time to drop by the newspaper's office to say hello."

Morgan chuckled. "To rub in her face the fact she was wrong about not only Locke Pointe, but also about reopening the Easton Island Airport?"

The airport's reopening had been a resounding success, garnering attention throughout the region. Including Michigan's governor and Ontario, Canada's premier in the official ribbon-cutting ceremony also hadn't hurt.

When questioned, Elizabeth neither confirmed nor denied having a hand in them showing up, but something told Morgan her grandmother had pulled a few strings to make it happen.

According to Denver Coates, the airport's manager, business was booming. They were adding flights daily, both arriving and departing, from the island's modern, state-of-the-art facility.

All in all, Morgan's life on Easton Island was perfect. Her ex-husband was in prison, still awaiting sentencing for kidnapping, robbing and assaulting her. With what little free time she had available, she spent it with her boyfriend, Wyatt Dawson, who was also one of Locke Village's patrol officers.

Morgan wasn't the only one staying busy. Her best friend helped manage Elizabeth's thriving art gallery down by the harbor. Her brother Brett, a savvy businessman, continued adding to the Easton family's portfolio.

It was almost too good to be true. Hence, another reason for her inkling of anxiety. Morgan's life had never, *ever* gone smoothly, at least not for a very long time.

Elizabeth interrupted her granddaughter's musings. "I believe I see Gerard and Randi's plane circling around now, getting ready to land."

The women stepped closer to the wall of windows, watching as the Gulfstream dipped down in front of the runway. It abruptly climbed again and an audible collective gasp could be heard from those waiting and watching.

"What is going on?" Morgan hissed under her breath. "I've never seen a plane almost touchdown, only to suddenly gain altitude again."

Elizabeth's hand shook as she removed her cell phone from her purse. "Let me text Denver to see if he knows why the plane gained altitude again."

She tapped the top of the screen. Seconds later, the reply came, not the one that Morgan had expected.

"Oh dear," her grandmother whispered. "There's a problem with the plane's landing gear."

Morgan could feel the blood drain from her face. Although she wasn't afraid of flying, several scenarios always stuck out in her mind when she took to the skies. One of them was emergency landings. In fact, she would listen for the landing gear, reassuring herself all was well and she would soon be on the ground.

A flicker of fear flitted across Elizabeth's face, quickly replaced by her standard, stoic expression. Not only was the archaeologist on board the charter flight, but her grandmother's close friend, Gerard Ainsworth, was flying in as well.

"I'm sure...I'm sure they'll figure it out." Morgan grasped her hand.

"Denver is up in the control tower," Elizabeth reminded her. "He's aware we're here waiting for this flight and invited us to join him. We'll have a better idea about what's happening from up there."

The women crossed the crowded terminal, passing by a handful of passengers seated near the gate staring at their phones, blissfully unaware of the scene unfolding.

Thankfully, the tower was a short walk, through a double set of steel doors, down a long corridor and up an elevator, only accessible with a special keycard, one of which Elizabeth had with her.

Morgan followed her grandmother into the control room. The air was electrified yet strangely quiet with all eyes focused on the skies.

Denver, who was watching for them, hurried over, a tense look on his face. "The pilot reported concerns about the landing gear before the plane left Toronto. They thought they'd resolved the issue, but apparently not."

"What exactly *is* the issue?" Morgan asked.

"They're not sure. It could be an electrical problem, a computer malfunction, or something else jamming it."

Elizabeth briefly closed her eyes, and Morgan could only imagine what was going through her mind. Her husband had died many years ago, during a return flight home to Easton Island. Was history repeating itself? Would this be another flight destined to take a tragic, devastating turn?

Morgan and Denver exchanged a quick glance, their faces mirroring the same feeling. And guilt crept in. Morgan and her brother were behind the airport's reopening, convincing the senior Easton it was the right decision.

How unbearable and unbelievable it would be for another person her grandmother cared deeply about to be taken away while flying. The idea made Morgan's stomach churn.

Her grandmother's voice was barely above a whisper. "What is the plan if they can't get the gear to engage?"

"Land without it."

"I see." Elizabeth grew quiet as the jet reappeared, circling once again.

Morgan clenched her jaw, silently praying for a miracle. *Please God. Please fix the landing gear.* In horror, she watched it pass by the control tower with no sign of the gear.

The staff at the controls huddled close together, talking in low voices.

Denver excused himself and joined them.

"Perhaps we should wait downstairs," Morgan gently suggested.

"Because you don't want me to see the plane hitting the ground and..." Elizabeth's voice trailed off. "We shall stay here and pray. Pray for a miracle."

The women joined hands, both closing their eyes. The only thing Morgan could do was to beg God for help.

Denver hurried back over. "They're coming in for a landing."

"And the gear?" Morgan asked.

"Is still not working. The plane will land without it."

Chapter 2

A slew of emergency vehicles...fire trucks, ambulances, police cars, all with their lights flashing, lined up along the side of the runway. The plane circled again and Morgan could only imagine what was running through the passengers' minds. Moments of sheer terror at knowing they would hit the ground, belly down, and then what?

She and her grandmother hovered off to the side, their eyes glued to the wall of windows. Lower and lower, the plane dipped. Morgan braced when it hit the runway. Sparks flew. The plane lifted slightly before hitting again, sending even more sparks flying.

As if in slow motion, the plane tipped to the side. For a horrifying moment, Morgan was certain it would start spinning like a top. Instead, it slowed until eventually coming to a halt near a strip of grass at the end of the runway.

As soon as it stopped moving, the emergency vehicles sped toward the aircraft. Things moved fast. The emergency door opened, and a slide appeared. One right after another, passengers slid to the ground and were immediately whisked away toward the terminal by emergency crew members.

Morgan leaned her arm against the cool glass, desperately trying to glimpse Gerard and Randi, safe and sound, but it was nearly impossible to pick them out. "Maybe we should go back downstairs."

Elizabeth caught Denver's eye. "Have you heard from the pilot or flight crew?"

"The pilot confirmed both crew and passengers are uninjured."

Elizabeth pressed a hand to her chest. "Thank God for an experienced pilot who kept his cool. Morgan and I will return downstairs to wait for our arrivals."

It was a quick trip down the elevator, along the concrete corridor, and through the double doors leading to the main terminal.

The scene was chaotic with people in a state of panic running back and forth, waiting for those on board the plane.

Embracing and crying when they caught sight of their loved ones, Morgan could feel the back of her eyes burn, knowing the terrifying incident could have ended tragically.

It seemed to take forever before Gerard, pale and visibly shaken, appeared.

"I see Gerard." Elizabeth stepped forward and lifted her hand.

He paused for a fraction of a second and strode over to where they stood waiting. "Quite an exciting landing, huh?"

"More like terrifying. Thank God you're all right." Elizabeth's voice shook. "You are all right?"

"Yes. Yes." Gerard cleared his throat. "I'm fine, although I'm sure the emergency landing took a few years off my life."

While they talked, a man in his sixties, if Morgan had to guess, appeared and stood quietly by Gerard's side. Out of the corner of her eye, she studied his sparse strands of gray hair poking out from beneath his ball cap, his silvery gray V-shaped goatee and wisps of hair dotting the curve of his ear.

"Randi?" she asked in a low voice.

"Randi for real. Richard for now." The man extended a slender hand. "Richard Spade. Pleasure to meet you," he said gruffly.

"Your costume is rather clever." Elizabeth's eyes traveled from the tip of the ball cap to the man's scuffed pair of steel-toed boots. "Except for the lack of an Adam's apple, you had me fooled. Whatever is wrong with your hands? Were you injured coming down the emergency slide?"

"No." Richard grimaced. "I'm having an allergic reaction to the glue that came in the packet of hand hair."

On closer inspection, Morgan noticed red welts forming on her hands. "You went to a lot of trouble to arrive disguised."

"I had no choice. I caught reporters spying on me last night when I left the hotel. Someone must have tipped them off."

"It wasn't Grandmother or me. We haven't breathed a word."

"I haven't told anyone," Gerard echoed.

"Perhaps your name was on the flight log," Elizabeth guessed.

"I'm sure it was." Richard frowned. "I wonder how long it will take for word to get back to the news crews tracking my moves."

"A crash landing won't help. I'm sure this will be all over the local stations later today," Elizabeth said. "Unfortunately, we'll need to wait for your bags."

"It might be a few minutes." Morgan shifted her gaze. Although no one else was sliding down the emergency slide, it was still surrounded by emergency staff. "They're probably checking to make sure it's safe to unload the bags."

Elizabeth casually glanced over her shoulder. "We're getting a bit of attention over by the vending machines."

Without turning her head, Morgan shifted her eyes, noting the two men gazing in their direction. "It could be someone who recognizes you, Grandmother."

Elizabeth shifted her purse. "Perhaps Denver can pull a few strings and grab the bags."

"Hang on. I see them unloading the luggage now," Morgan said. "It probably won't take long."

Another half hour passed, with the terminal becoming even more crowded while passengers continued waiting.

Finally, there was an announcement that both checked bags and carry-on luggage were available on the carousel.

Morgan removed her keys from her pocket. "While you grab the bags, I'll bring the car around."

She reached her SUV and circled the parking lot, pulling up alongside the terminal where Elizabeth and their guests stood waiting. She hopped out and helped them load the luggage before sliding behind the wheel. "Because Easton Estate is on our way, we'll drop Grandmother and Gerard off first."

Randi rubbed her hands together. "At the risk of sounding snoopy, do you mind if I take a quick tour? I was killing time at the airport during our delay and found some interesting stories about the Easton Estate. It sounds like some swanky digs."

"Morgan can give you a tour," Elizabeth said. "The only area off limits is my private apartment. I'm doing some deep cleaning, so it's not suitable for entertaining guests."

Morgan bit back a reply, reminding her grandmother she'd been cleaning for several months. In fact, she'd packed up several boxes of mementos and art pieces which held sentimental value, insisting she wanted her granddaughter to have them.

From what Brett, had told her, he'd been on the receiving end of several heirlooms, as well.

When pressed, Elizabeth claimed she was de-cluttering and simplifying her life. To Morgan, it was a sad reminder her grandmother wouldn't be around forever and was preparing for her eventual passing.

"We'll do a quick tour of the grounds and house." The trip there flew by and soon Morgan pulled through the gates, along the winding driveway until the sprawling estate appeared.

"Good gravy." Randi let out a low whistle. "The photos don't do this place justice. It's almost as big as Buckingham Palace."

"Not quite. I believe Buckingham Palace has several hundred rooms. Easton Estate is a shack compared to the palace."

"You're being way too modest," Gerard said. "This is an exquisite piece of property."

"It's home." Elizabeth shrugged. "I suppose to some, it would appear stately."

"I bet this place is worth a pretty penny," Randi said. "The information I found only gave ballpark figures of the cost."

"I don't discuss money," Elizabeth gently reprimanded. "I've relinquished my responsibilities and leave decisions about expenses and assets to my grandchildren."

Morgan parked alongside the garage and hopped out. She ran around to give her grandmother a hand while Randi and Gerard exited the back.

"I've arranged for tea in the library for Gerard and me." Elizabeth's brows furrowed. "At least I believe I asked Mrs. Arnsby to have tea ready."

Clearly, Elizabeth was still shaken over watching the emergency landing, which was quickly confirmed when Morgan noticed her hand shaking when she reached for the door handle. "You did. I remember you mentioning it to me. Let me show Gerard and Randi to the library. I need a minute of your time before giving Randi a tour."

Morgan led their guests inside and caught up with her grandmother in the hallway. "I think we could both use a minute to catch our breaths."

"Yes. Thank you, dear. I'm still rattled over the plane's emergency landing."

Morgan grasped her elbow and guided her to the office at the other end of the hall. She quietly closed the door behind them.

As soon as the door shut, her grandmother slumped in the chair and leaned her head back. "I can still see the plane and sparks flying when I close my eyes."

Morgan knelt next to her. "I can only imagine what was going through your mind."

"About Garrett's death. Maybe this was God's way of reminding me."

"Reminding you of what?"

"It's in my best interest not to get too close to people."

"Surely, you can't believe that," Morgan argued. "You care for Mr. Ainsworth."

Her grandmother lifted her head, offering her a hesitant smile. "More than I've cared to admit for a long time."

"What's holding you back?"

"Honestly?"

Morgan nodded.

"Heartbreak. Garrett's death nearly destroyed me. I vowed I would never love another man so deeply."

"But you did...fall in love again," Morgan said softly. "I can see it in your eyes."

A small sigh escaped Elizabeth's lips. "Is it so obvious?"

"To me, it is." Morgan hesitated. Was her grandmother ready for what she had to say? There was only one way to find out. "I can tell by the way Mr. Ainsworth looks at you, he feels the same."

Elizabeth tilted her head, eyeing her granddaughter thoughtfully. "Do you think so?"

"I know so. He's in love with you."

"Love is complicated."

"Is it?"

"He has his life. I have mine."

"And you see no way to create a new life together?" Morgan leveled her gaze.

"You're giving me the look."

"Because you can mingle lives, mingle families. People do it every day. I can't count the number of times you drilled into my head not to let what Jason did to me make me bitter and afraid to love someone again."

"There's a big difference in our situations. You're young. I'm old."

"Age is an excuse, and a poor one at that."

Elizabeth grinned. "You're getting cheeky, young lady."

"Only because I love you." Morgan gave her grandmother a gentle hug before offering her a hand up. "Now, get in there and know that what happened earlier was God's reminder we only have one life to live. Embrace and enjoy every minute of it."

Chapter 3

Morgan and Elizabeth stepped into the library where they found Richard and Gerard near the window, talking in low voices. "I hope we didn't keep you," Elizabeth said.

"Not at all." Gerard crossed the room. "We were admiring Easton Estate's picturesque grounds. Actually, we were remarking about how happy we were to be *on the ground*."

"I can only imagine. Randi...Richard and I will take a brief tour and head out. We'll see you later for dinner." Morgan gave her grandmother a sly wink, to which Elizabeth rolled her eyes, but there was a smile on her face.

"Shall we?" Morgan led her guest out of the library, passing by Mrs. Arnsby, who was steering a tea cart down the long hall. "Hello, Morgan. Will you be having tea with your grandmother and her friend?"

"Not this time." She made a brief introduction. "I'm giving my guest a quick tour of Easton Estate and then we'll be heading over to Locke Pointe."

An odd expression flickered across the cook's face as she shook Richard's hand. "Are you staying at Locke Pointe Bed-and-Breakfast?"

"For a few days. I've never visited the island before." Richard sniffled loudly. "I was wondering if I might use your restroom."

"It's down the hall and on the right." Mrs. Arnsby waited until he was out of earshot. "I'm getting a funny feeling about your new guest," she whispered. "How long have you known him?"

"A few months. Grandmother's friend, Gerard, introduced us. What kind of funny feeling?" Morgan asked.

"Like something's off." Mrs. Arnsby's brows knitted. "Maybe it's because he's pale and thin."

"Richard is a little on the thin side. Perhaps we should try fattening him up while he's here."

"It's not only his appearance. I can't quite put my finger on it. He strikes me as a little odd."

"There's no need to worry. Grandmother and Gerard would never allow someone to stay with me if they had even an inkling of concern."

"True." The woman relaxed her stance. "Considering all you've been through, perhaps I'm just being overly cautious."

Morgan gave her a quick hug. "Thank you for worrying about me. I promise, I'm safe."

Richard reappeared, and their conversation ended with Mrs. Arnsby making her way to the library, while Morgan began what she thought would be a short tour of the lower level. She quickly discovered she was mistaken.

Randi was an inquisitive individual. They spent a great deal of time in the downstairs office with the woman asking several questions about works of art and various awards honoring Garrett Easton's accomplishments.

"Honestly, I only know what I've read or what Grandmother and Brett have told me," Morgan finally said. "I grew up in Florida and don't remember my grandfather."

Randi's expression grew thoughtful. "I know the story, in a roundabout way. It must have been tough."

"Actually, it was the exact opposite. My childhood was a breeze. On the flip side, my mother's death was devastating. Finding out about Easton Island and my family was a shock."

"Yet here you are. The human spirit is amazing, how someone can endure catastrophic loss, eventually heal, and move forward."

"It didn't happen overnight," Morgan said. "I still grieve the loss of my mother, but I also often feel her presence."

"Because a part of her is still here, still on the island."

"Precisely." Morgan made brief stops in her upstairs office, her bedroom and a few of the other guest rooms, careful to steer clear of the north wing and her grandmother's apartment.

They returned to the top of the stairs and Randi abruptly stopped, motioning across the open expanse to Elizabeth's wing on the opposite side. "Is that your grandmother's place?"

"It is."

"She has an entire wing of the house to herself?"

"Yes. Brett spends part of his time at the Toronto penthouse. I have my own home. She could turn this entire floor into her apartment if she wanted to."

Randi leaned in and lowered her voice. "I have a confession."

"A confession?"

"Mrs. Easton can be a little intimidating."

A slow smile spread across Morgan's face. "She can. When needed, Grandmother is as tough as nails. She's also the most extraordinary, interesting and wonderful person I have ever met in my life."

Randi's eyes met Morgan's. "You two are close."

"We are. I can't imagine where I would be right now if not for her."

"Which makes her, you, and the Easton family even more intriguing. Everyone loves a hero, loves to hear about families sticking together and having each other's backs." Randi reached for the railing. "Something tells me I'm going to enjoy my visit to Easton Island immensely."

Chapter 4

"Let me help you with your bags." Morgan caught up with Randi near the rear of her SUV and made a move to grab the woman's carry-on.

"Hold up!" Randi lunged forward. "I'll handle this one."

"What's in there...dynamite?" Morgan joked.

"Some very delicate and important items, several of them needed for the authentication."

"Duly noted. It's all yours." Morgan slid the second bag to the edge of the cargo area. Underestimating the weight, she hoisted it up and nearly dropped it. "This thing weighs a ton."

"I should have mentioned my other bag is a little heavy."

"A little heavy?" Morgan grabbed the handle and tried lifting it. Using both hands, she finally cleared her cargo area. "What do you have in here?" she groaned. "A bag of bricks?"

"Some extra gear." Randi pursed her lips. "I try to pack light, although it rarely works out. You never know what you might need during exploration or research."

Morgan extended the handle and began wheeling it across the paved parking lot. "There's no way I'll be able to drag this thing up a flight of stairs," she gasped. "We're going to have to take the elevator."

While she walked, Morgan rattled off a few of Locke Pointe's highlights, making sure she mentioned the breakfast and social hour schedule. She reached the entrance to the elevator and realized she'd lost her guest, who now stood several steps behind her, staring up.

She left the bag near the elevator doors and returned to the woman's side. "Is everything all right?"

"Fine. Fabulous. I'm admiring the exterior. This home is an excellent example of Victorian architecture with a hint of contemporary styling."

Morgan pivoted, critiquing the estate from Randi's perspective. "You have a good eye and are one hundred percent correct. The outside has Victorian influences while the inside is...well, you'll see in a minute."

"Those half-moon windows are intriguing. It's almost as if they're keeping watch over the property."

"My grandparents were very strategic about Locke Pointe's design." Morgan was on the fence about telling the woman exactly how she'd found the medallion, but if she trusted her enough to show it to her, what harm was there in telling Randi how she'd found it? "They're significant, and I'll tell you why when I give you a tour."

"I can't wait." Randi fell into step. "Do you think my disguise is overkill?"

"Overkill?"

"You know...over the top."

Morgan thought about it. "I don't know if I would call it overkill, but I have to admit, I'm not sure how you're going to pull it off for any length of time."

"It's my voice, isn't it?"

"Your voice and." Morgan motioned to the woman's bare arm. "I hate to be Debbie Downer, but your arm hair looks fake."

"It's also itchy."

"I appreciate the time and effort you put into making sure word doesn't get out you're on Easton Island, but I don't want you feeling uncomfortable during your stay," Morgan said. "I'm thrilled you're here and eager for you to examine the medallion.

Having said that, I also want you to enjoy your visit."

"I appreciate your concern. I have to admit, from what I've seen so far, the island is charming and unique."

"More than charming. I may be biased, but I think it's perfect and can't imagine living anywhere else."

The elevator reached the upper floor. The doors opened and Morgan strolled down the hall with her guest hustling to keep up. "You'll be staying in my Somewhere in Time suite. It overlooks the rear of the property along with a peek-a-boo view of the Lilac Inn, my friend and inn owner Grace Coates' place."

"Somewhere in Time," Randi repeated. "There was a popular movie some years ago, set on a well-known island not far from here called Somewhere in Time."

"Mackinac Island." Morgan removed the suite's keycard from her pocket. "I haven't visited it yet, but it's on my to-do list."

"You really should check it out. Mackinac reminds me of this island based on what I've seen so far."

"I've heard similar comments before." Morgan swung the suite's door open and stepped inside. "You'll find a small coffeemaker counter in the corner, along with a welcome basket. The bathroom is fully stocked. If you find you're missing something, let me know."

Randi dropped her bag near the door and slowly circled the room. She placed her hand on the bed and lightly pressed down. "The mattress is nice and firm, just the way I like it."

Morgan watched her meander over to the side table and inspect the lamp. "That is a tiffany lamp. There's one in each suite."

"You have excellent taste."

"Not me. My grandparents had excellent taste," Morgan corrected. "A fair number of the furnishings belonged to them and were here when I inherited the property."

Randi spun around. "I can't imagine someone leaving me an exquisite estate like this."

"The property comes with its own set of unique challenges and lingering reminders of my losses."

"I'm sorry," the woman apologized. "I didn't mean to diminish your loss with my ramblings."

"It's all right. Although I've been through a lot and miss my mom, I also gained a great deal." Morgan changed the subject. "Do the accommodations meet your approval?"

Randi gave her a double thumbs up. "This place is way nicer than some of the places I've stayed."

"I bet. I'll give you time to unpack and settle in." Morgan glanced at her watch. "After you finish, we can tour the property."

"Sounds good."

Morgan quietly closed the door behind her and returned to the main floor. Chester, her pup, met her at the bottom of the stairs.

"Hey buddy." She playfully tweaked his ear. "You had no idea I sneaked in on the elevator, did you?"

Chester pranced in circles, his tail wagging wildly, acting as if she'd been gone for days, not just a couple of hours. "Let's go see what Tina's up to."

She and her pup wandered into the kitchen where they found the cook standing at the counter, surrounded by mixing bowls and baking dishes.

"You're back."

"Our new guest is settling in. Is there anything I can help you with?"

"Thanks for the offer. Despite the clutter and chaos, I believe I have it under control." Tina grabbed the edge of her apron and wiped her hands. "How do margarita flatbread pizzas sound for this afternoon's social hour?"

"I love flatbread pizzas."

"I figured we could serve those, along with some baked chicken wings, celery and blue cheese dressing."

"It sounds delicious. I'm sure our guests will love whatever you serve." Not long ago Tina had confessed to Morgan she almost turned down her job offer, claiming she was burned out after years of working as a line cook. Curious about Locke Pointe, she met Morgan at the property with the intention of telling her she wasn't interested.

It was only later Morgan found out that the moment Tina stepped foot inside Locke Pointe she changed her mind, claiming she'd been enveloped in a sense of peace, as if she was meant to be there.

Morgan knew exactly how the woman felt. Locke Pointe had a way of drawing you in, filling you with a sense of comfort, warmth, and belonging. Since opening her doors and welcoming guests, she'd heard similar comments again and again.

Locke Pointe had found its purpose, had embraced it and given guests exactly what they needed. A sanctuary, a retreat far away from the hustle and bustle of a busy world.

"You keep doing your thing and our guests will keep coming back."

TING...Ting...ting...ting...ting, ting, ting. The front doorbell chimed. "Now, who could that be?" Morgan hustled out of the kitchen, through the dining room and to the front door.

Peering through the stained glass panels, she could see someone standing on her front porch. She eased the door open, coming face to face with a stranger, yet someone who looked vaguely familiar.

Chapter 5

"I've finished unpacking." Gerard joined Elizabeth, who stood waiting for him at the bottom of the main staircase. "The room and attached bath are exquisitely appointed. You must have given me the grand suite," he teased.

"Perhaps." Elizabeth winked. "A few of the rooms were recently refreshed. I'm happy to hear it meets your approval."

"More than meets my approval." Gerard lifted her hand and placed a light kiss on top. "Have I ever told you how beautiful you are? You get lovelier every time we meet."

Elizabeth attempted a stern expression, failing miserably. "Stop with your nonsense. I'm old and wrinkly."

"I wholeheartedly disagree. I see nothing but the beautiful young woman I met to discuss art all those years ago." He crooked his elbow, offering her his arm. "It's a beautiful day. The sun is shining. Could I perhaps persuade you to accompany me for a leisurely walk around the grounds?"

"Persuade away."

The couple strolled arm-in-arm, to the end of the hall and out the back door, which opened to an expansive paved patio. The walkway looped in a wide arch, meandering past the main garage, a second separate garage which housed the estate's rare and valuable vehicles, followed by Jax's workshop.

While they walked, Elizabeth rattled off some of the recent renovations. "It's a massive estate and always in need of upkeep."

"Massive estate with only one person living here, other than the staff," Gerard pointed out.

"True, although Brett is here often."

"But not Morgan."

"She has her own home. Looking Glass Cottage is only a short drive away."

"She hasn't moved into Locke Pointe?"

"No, and she has no plans to do so. Morgan prefers the smaller home. She and Quinn both live there."

"Who is running the bed-and-breakfast?"

"Morgan and Ronni Lansbury, Laura's close friend."

"Morgan's mother's friend?"

"Correct."

Gerard slowed. "I suppose we drifted a little off topic."

"We have?"

"We were discussing Easton Estate and how you live alone. Have you ever considered downsizing and perhaps moving to the city?" he hinted.

"As in Toronto?" Elizabeth tightened her grip on his arm. "I see now where this conversation is going. I'm content spending the rest of my days living on Easton Island. Morgan is here. As I mentioned, Brett is often here. It's home."

"I thought as much, but figured it wouldn't hurt to ask."

"What about you?" Elizabeth shot him a side glance. "Have you ever considered moving out of the city?"

"I have and would do so for the right reasons," Gerard said.

"Which are?"

The couple reached a row of meticulously manicured bushes with a park bench strategically situated in the center. The greenery gave them privacy on one side, while offering them an unobstructed view of Lake Huron on the other.

"Shall we sit and enjoy the view?" Gerard led Elizabeth to the bench and waited for her to have a seat. "I would move if I had the chance to spend the rest of my life with the woman I loved."

Elizabeth caught his eye. The meaning of his words was crystal clear. "We're up there in years, Gerard."

"But not so old that we don't deserve another chance at love," he said. "I almost convinced you to fall in love with me years ago and am ready to try again."

"Who said you didn't succeed?" she asked.

Gerard's expression grew hopeful. "If I recall correctly, you weren't interested in a relationship. I thought..."

Elizabeth squeezed his hand. "The timing was off. Looking back, I wasn't ready."

"Are you saying maybe you're open to me courting you again?"

"Courting sounds so old-fashioned."

"You just said we were old," he teased. "Let me rephrase my line of questioning. You're open to dating again?"

"Perhaps. My granddaughter not so subtly reminded me we only have one life. When your plane..." Elizabeth's voice trailed off. "I was terrified."

"I'm sorry you had to be there to watch the emergency landing."

"Skidding down the runway with sparks flying. All I could think about was the plane bursting into flames and knowing you were inside." Elizabeth looked away, unable to continue.

"Perhaps it was God's way of letting you know you care...about me."

"I have always cared about you, more than you know." She sucked in a breath. "I'm open to dating again."

Gerard's eyes lit. "This is music to my ears." He leaned in and gently kissed her cheek. "There are a million things we could do, places we could go. I can't tell you how thrilled I was to discover you're flying again. You could come to Toronto and stay with me. We could catch some Broadway shows. I know how much you adore French cuisine. There's a lovely little bistro a short walk from my apartment..."

Elizabeth lifted her hand. "We'll need to start with a first date before planning weekend getaways."

"True. We'll embark on our first official date here on the island. A local seated next to me on the plane told me about a fantastic restaurant in Easton Harbor serving French cuisine. I would love to take you there this evening."

"Unfortunately, Morgan, Randi, Brett and Quinn will be here for dinner so that Randi can examine the medallion."

"You're right. I got so excited, I forgot. Tomorrow night, then."

"Tomorrow night, it is," Elizabeth agreed. "Speaking of Randi and Morgan, I wonder how they're getting on."

"I know Randi was excited to visit Easton Island."

"You two came in on the same flight. Has she been staying in the area for some other work project?"

"No. She's been on a brief break," Gerard said.

"You two must be close. I remember her specifically telling Morgan and me she rarely agrees to meet with strangers."

"It's true. Randi is an introverted extrovert, if that makes sense."

"Based on what I know about her, I could see her being some of both." Elizabeth sensed a slight hesitation on Gerard's part when talking about the archaeologist. There was something else, something he wasn't saying. "I don't believe you ever told me how you two met."

"I haven't." Gerard shifted slightly, tugging at the edge of his collar.

"I can tell by your reaction there's something about her you haven't shared."

"There is. If we're moving our relationship up a notch and dating, I need to come clean about Randi."

Chapter 6

"Can I help you?" Morgan studied the blonde standing on Locke Pointe's front porch, her eyes narrowing.

"I was wondering if I could speak with the owner."

"About what?"

"Window washing."

"I don't need my windows washed." Morgan started to close the door.

The woman blocked her by wedging her foot in the opening. "You don't know who I am?"

"No. Should I?"

The stranger lifted the corner of her wig, revealing wisps of curly brown hair. "It's me," she whispered in a low voice.

Morgan leaned in. "Randi?"

"But now Lynn."

"What happened to…"

"Richard? I decided to switch over to my backup plan and use my middle name, Lynn."

"Which is probably not a bad idea. I'm almost positive I would have trouble explaining to my staff how Richard became Lynn."

Chester, who had followed Morgan to the front door, scooted past her and began sniffing the woman's leg.

"This is Chester, my best bud, and the inn's unofficial mascot."

"Hello, Chester." Randi rubbed his ears and patted his back. "He's a friendly fellow."

"Unless you're giving off bad vibes," Morgan said. "Chester is protective of me."

"I would love to have a dog. Maybe someday when I settle down." Randi straightened her back. "So, you didn't recognize me?"

"You looked kinda familiar, although the blond wig threw me off."

"Cool."

"Let me guess...you're Lynn with a last name of Spade, which is the one Grandmother told me to use to reserve your room."

Randi made a digging motion. "Spade, as in excavating. Get it?"

"I'm glad you retired Richard."

"Me too. I've always wanted to try a male disguise and now I know it won't work. At least, not for me." Randi followed Morgan into the house, scratching the side of her face. "The facial hair was starting to give me hives."

"You look a little blotchy and bumpy. There's a tube of moisturizing cream, made in Michigan, in your bathroom. It might help if you slathered some on."

"Already used it. I can't wait to try the other goodies I found in the basket...the gourmet coffee, Mackinac Island fudge, the cookies."

"I'm happy to hear the suite is working out." Morgan dusted her hands. "I figured we could start the tour on the main floor and work our way up."

"Lead the way." Randi followed Morgan and Chester into the kitchen. "I'm not sure if I asked before, but is this your home, too?"

"No. I live in a small cottage not far from here." Morgan eased the kitchen door open and stepped aside. "Welcome to the heart of Locke Pointe Bed-and-Breakfast, the kitchen."

Randi's jaw dropped. "Rockin' retro."

"Or maybe a better word would be vintage," Morgan quipped.

"I feel like I stepped onto the Brady Bunch studio where no one ever cooked because the kitchen was only for looks."

Morgan motioned to the woman standing at the counter. "Lynn, this is Tina. She's the one who whips up all of Locke Pointe's delicious dishes."

Tina stepped around the center island and held out her hand. "It's nice to meet you. This kitchen may look messy, but I can assure you it's one hundred percent organized chaos."

"I think it's sweet and pretty cool myself."

"Tina, meet our new guest, Lynn Spade. She'll only be here for a couple of days."

"Welcome to Locke Pointe. I hope you enjoy your stay."

The women continued their tour, stopping by the office where they found Ronni seated at the desk, staring intently at her laptop's screen.

"Knock, knock."

"Morgan." Ronni sprang from her chair. "You're back with our new guest."

"Ronni Lansbury, this is Lynn Spade."

The women made small talk until Ronni's cell phone rang and she excused herself.

On the way out, Lynn paused to take a closer look at the prestigious awards and plaques lining the walls. "Your grandfather studied astronomy?"

"He did. In fact, I believe my grandparents designed Locke Pointe with studying the stars in mind." Continuing their tour, Morgan led her through the bright and airy three-season porch offering views of the backyard and Lake Huron.

"This place is like a breath of fresh air," Randi said. "It's hard to believe it sat empty for so many years."

"Empty, sad and forlorn, but not any longer." Morgan's next stop was the large, open living room.

Randi tucked her hands behind her back and gazed out the window. "The view is spectacular. I could sit here for hours."

"It's a peaceful place." Morgan watched her guest cross the room and stop when she reached the fireplace.

"The painting of Locke Pointe is incredible. The artist put a great deal of effort into the details." Randi pivoted. "Do you know who painted this?"

"I do. It was my mom, although I wasn't around at the time or don't remember her working on it. I'm sure it was a labor of love."

Randi admired a few more pieces of art strategically placed around the room before the women trekked up the stairs to the second floor.

"Several of the suites are occupied, so I can't show you those. ME's suite, which stands for Morgan and Elizabeth, is unoccupied." Morgan escorted her to the end of the long hall. Using her main keycard, she opened the door and motioned the woman inside.

"Sweet suite. This is first class luxury all the way." Randi ran a light hand over a delicate doily Morgan had found tucked away in one of the dresser drawers. "I'm impressed. You kept true to the history of the place, down to the smallest of details."

"I changed as little as possible, including the kitchen."

"Which is pretty awesome, if you ask me."

"Thank you. I think my grandparents would approve." Morgan crossed the room, following Chester, who had already made a beeline for his favorite spot, the bathroom shower.

Randi trailed behind. "Talk about a luxurious spa bath. I wouldn't mind soaking in the jetted tub for a day or three."

"I'm not sure if it's booked. I know someone was inquiring about pricing."

"I was kidding, although it is very nice." Randi peered into the shower. "Your dog digs the shower."

"It's his favorite spot in the house."

"He likes baths?" Randi grinned.

"Actually, Chester hates them. I don't think he realizes what the shower is for, at least not yet."

The woman slipped in behind the glass enclosure, her attention focused on the star pattern, the key to unlocking the door leading to the third floor. It had been several days since Morgan's last check of the space, mainly because there was no way to access it when guests were staying in ME's suite.

Although it hadn't been a problem, considering nothing was up there except for a few storage boxes. Everything of value had been removed. At least Morgan believed it was empty.

Randi ran the tip of her finger along the edge, tracing the outline of the star. "This reminds me of the North Star." She grew quiet, continuing to study the detailed pattern, and Morgan could see her wheels were spinning. "You've seen the star pattern before."

"I have. It was in your mother's painting of Locke Pointe." Randi's hand fell to her side. She stepped out of the shower, a thoughtful expression on her face. "There's some sort of significance to this pattern and the painting. Your grandfather studied astronomy. This all means something, which is why you wanted to show this room to me."

"I did."

"What does the star mean?"

Morgan sucked in a breath as an internal battle waged...had been waging from the moment Randi Colbane had agreed to travel to Easton Island to authenticate the Shifting Sands Medallion.

Could she trust the woman, tell her all she knew, how she had found the potentially priceless artifact? The most important question was...would it help for the Biblical archaeologist to hear how Morgan had finally solved the mystery?

"Actually, the shower's star pattern and my mom's Locke Pointe painting helped me find the medallion."

Chapter 7

"Wait here. I'll be right back." Morgan ran downstairs to the office, breathing a sigh of relief when she discovered Ronni was no longer there, although her laptop was open and the screen still lit.

She slid the portrait of her grandparents aside, revealing the estate's hidden safe. With a quick glance over her shoulder, she entered the access code and opened the door. Reaching inside, she removed the gem-encrusted star, which sat on top of a box of old coins she'd recently found.

Although Morgan believed the safe was secure and she'd briefly considered placing the medallion inside, she decided against it, mainly because Easton Estate's safe was virtually indestructible. There was also the fact guests were continually coming and going from Locke Pointe. All it would take was for an inquisitive guest to start snooping around. Besides, she already had enough on her mind to keep her up at night.

The star key was a different story. Even if a guest or an employee found the safe and managed to "crack the code," at first glance, it appeared to be nothing more than a trinket with little value.

She returned upstairs to find Randi still standing in the shower. "This wall has a gap in it."

"It does, and you'll find out why in a minute." Morgan waited for the woman to step aside before placing the star in the cutout. She gently twisted it. The door silently opened, revealing a set of stairs.

"Check it out," Randi gasped. "I feel a little like Indiana Jones and the Temple of Doom. Where did you get the key?"

"I found it in a secret closet inside Looking Glass Cottage's main bedroom."

"And you noticed it matched the cutout here in the shower?"

"I did, although it took a while for me to figure it out. I found the key before inheriting this property in December."

Randi rubbed her palms together. "I'm ready to explore."

"Don't get too excited," Morgan warned. "There's not much upstairs, just some boxes of stuff I probably need to toss."

The women climbed the steps and turned left, entering the first room.

Randi poked around in the boxes before stacking them back on top of each other. "You're right. It's almost empty. The rolling metal doors are an interesting addition. The catwalk looks as if it was used to transport stuff from one side to the other."

"I was thinking the same thing, although I have no idea what it could have been." Morgan followed Randi into the hall, watching as she knelt on the floor and lightly ran her fingertips across the boards. "What are you doing?"

"There are grooves in the wood, like maybe they had some sort of heavy cart."

Morgan dropped to her knees and pressed her palm against the boards. "I never noticed them before. Good eye."

"That's why they pay me the big bucks," Randi joked. "So, what's in the other room?"

"A few more boxes."

"Which means your sparkly key, the painting downstairs, and the secret door is much ado about nothing."

"Not quite." Morgan sprang to her feet. "Follow me."

Chester, who had been trailing behind, trotted past them and flopped down on the exact spot Morgan planned to show Randi...the hidden space beneath the floorboards. "You're such a nutty dog," she said. "You'll have to move in a minute."

Her pup lowered his head, resting it on his front paw while he watched the women step in front of the half-moon windows.

"This is an interesting view," Randi remarked.

"I found the medallion in here, on December twenty-first, the beginning of the winter solstice between ten and eleven at night."

The woman arched a brow. "You remember the exact day and time? I'm impressed."

"There's a reason." Morgan filled her in, starting again with finding the star and discovering it fit inside the shower wall.

"How does your mother's painting fit in?" Randi asked.

"I found a slip of paper with two sets of numbers hidden behind the frame. Twelve twenty-one and twenty-two, twenty-three."

"Ah." The woman spun in a slow circle. "You figured out the first numbers were the day, and the second was military time, between ten and eleven p.m."

"Yep."

"I love a good mystery. After figuring it out, you came up here on that date in December and found the medallion...where?"

Morgan stood in front of the window and made a downward motion. "Imagine a clear night with the moon shining down through the window and onto this floor."

Randi's eyes grew round as saucers. "With a star, matching the one in the shower, the key, and in your mother's painting."

Morgan removed the star key from her pocket and set it on the floor. "The moon's light filters in through here, casting a star pattern, identical to this key, at almost eleven."

The woman let out a low whistle. "Indiana Jones ain't got nothing on you."

"I had a little help from my boyfriend, Wyatt."

"Can you show me exactly where you found it?"

"Sure. As soon as I can convince Chester to move. C'mon, buddy." Morgan nudged him with her foot. "You're on the spot."

Her pup, in no hurry to vacate his current location, refused to budge, forcing Morgan to slide him across the dusty floor.

"Your dog has a mind of his own," Randi laughed. "He's giving you a make-me-move look."

"Chester is one of the most intelligent dogs I've ever had. He's smart, maybe too smart, for his own britches, and will not hesitate to share his feelings if you do something he doesn't like, especially dress him up in cute clothes which make him look adorable." Morgan patted his side. "Isn't that right?"

Chester's ears flattened. He gave her an annoyed look before reluctantly vacating his location and trotting out of the room.

Randi placed her hands on her hips. "He showed you who's boss."

"Every day. You'll never meet a more loyal and loving companion than my Chester." Morgan turned her attention to the spot. "Crud. I forgot to bring a flathead screwdriver with me."

"I have one." Randi reached into her pocket. She pulled out a bright red multi-purpose pocket tool and handed it to Morgan. "This little gem is one of the best twenty-dollar investments I ever made."

"Thank you." Morgan gave it the once over before easing the tip into the board she thought was the right one.

It refused to budge. "This might take a minute."

She rolled back on her heels and gazed out the window. "It would help if it was December twenty-first and ten at night. I'm in the general vicinity, though. The exact spot is around here somewhere."

With Randi's help, the women began examining the floorboards, searching for a small gap—any indication that a board was loose. They spent several long moments poking, prying, and searching.

Morgan's calves started to ache. She eased onto her backside and began massaging her sore muscles. "It was so much easier last time."

"The hiding spot has to be here somewhere." Randi continued poking and prying. "I found a board that seems to have a little give."

"You'll need this." Morgan handed her the multi-tool, watching as the woman gently eased the flathead screwdriver along the seam.

Pop.

The board popped out.

Morgan helped her remove the rest of the boards, revealing the empty spot where the box, along with a family photo album, had once been safely tucked away.

"Most people would never have found this." Randi snapped the screwdriver back in place and tucked the tool in her pocket. "Was the medallion sitting on top, or was it in some sort of box?"

"It was in a box." Morgan turned her cell phone on and scrolled through the screen until she found the picture of the tarnished brass box with the words *Shifting Sands Medallion* etched on top.

"Can I see the photo of the medallion?"

Morgan scrolled again until she found the picture she'd taken, the one she and her grandmother had shown Randi when they met her for lunch in Port Huron.

"I have to admit, if this is authentic, I'm amazed at the excellent condition it's in. Although looking at the box, it appears to have been well preserved. Whoever placed it in the special box knew what they were doing."

"It was my grandparents, my mother, or whoever gave it to them."

Randi handed the phone back. "Where is it now? Here at Locke Pointe?"

Morgan shook her head. "I wouldn't be able to sleep at night if I left it here."

"I don't blame you." Randi crossed her legs. "It doesn't matter where it is, as long as it's in a safe place. When can I see it?"

"Tonight, after dinner. We're having dinner at Easton Estate."

Randi made a clicking sound with her teeth. "This is a pretty sizeable space for a small box and photo album."

"It's possible my grandparents hid other stuff down there at one time."

"Do you mind?"

"Mind what?"

"If I take a closer look."

"Be my guest."

"Thanks." Randi turned her cell phone's flashlight on. The bright light beamed in the dark hole and Morgan quietly listened to the woman carry on a one-sided conversation.

"...such an intriguing mystery. The star, the painting, the secret door. I'm liking Easton Island more by the minute." Randi abruptly slid back and began fumbling inside her pocket. "Awesome sauce."

Chapter 8

Morgan scrambled across the floor. "You found something else in the hiding spot? How is that even possible? Wyatt and I searched every nook and cranny."

Randi wiggled farther into the opening, her cell phone's light bobbing up and down. She began humming under her breath. The humming mingled with a *tink, tink* sound.

Morgan craned her neck. "Is there anything I can do to help? Maybe I can go grab a flashlight."

The woman flew forward, nearly colliding with her. "Psych!"

"What the..." Morgan stumbled back, clutching her chest.

"Sorry. I couldn't resist. There's nothing else down there. I was just messing with you."

"Nothing?"

"Nope." Randi wiped her hands on her cargo shorts. "It's clean as a whistle and a very clever hiding spot, I might add. Is there any chance I can check it out at night?"

"We'll have to play it by ear." Morgan explained she would need to check to see if guests had reserved the main suite. "I'll have to figure out when it will be unoccupied. If we didn't already have plans for this evening, we could check it out later."

"Bummer. It's not relevant to my authentication process. I just thought it would be cool to see the star's reflection." Working together, Randi and Morgan replaced the floorboards and then trekked down the stairs.

"I was thinking I might like to take a look around the grounds."

"We can start out back." Morgan led her to the recently added firepit and Adirondack chairs. They made a quick stop at the carriage house, where Morgan showed her the bikes available for guests to use before meandering across the yard and down the steep slope toward the water's edge.

Randi grew quiet, gazing out across Lake Huron's wide expanse, where there was nothing but waves and water for as far as the eye could see.

"I'm sure you've seen some cool stuff over the years. How does this view compare?" Morgan finally asked.

"It's stunning." Randi closed her eyes and took a deep breath. "I could do this."

"Do what?"

"Live here. Live on an island surrounded by all of this natural beauty. Embrace a change of pace."

"It's like a whole other world." Morgan confided she had no plans to move to Easton Island after learning about it. "I was going to stay long enough for the reading of my mother's will and then hightail it back to Florida."

The woman's eyes flew open. "But when you got here, the island had different ideas. It cast a spell on you."

"Maybe not a spell, but it captured my heart." A slow smile spread across Morgan's face at the memory. "I always thought Fort Myers was my forever home until I got here and everything changed."

"You're a lucky woman, Morgan Easton."

"Blessed. I'm blessed beyond belief," Morgan said. "God had other plans for me and I couldn't be more grateful."

The women made their way along the shoreline while Morgan told her guest about the kayaks and canoes. "There's a sign-up / sign-out sheet on a clipboard inside the door. If you take the equipment out, be sure to jot down the time you left."

"In case something happens, and a guest goes missing. You'll know when they left."

"Correct."

"Good idea. It would be easy to get in trouble."

"Or become stranded on a deserted island after your kayak floats away while you weren't looking."

Randi arched a brow. "Someone you know?"

"Yeah. Me and my friend Quinn. We borrowed a kayak from Easton Estate, didn't bother telling anyone where we were going, and ended up stranded on Bird Island."

"You didn't have your cell phones with you?"

"We had them. What we didn't have was cell reception. Thankfully, enough people noticed we were missing and sent out a search party."

The women returned to the storage building. Morgan started to climb the steep hill when Randi stopped her. "Hold up."

Starting at the water's edge, she counted out the paces to the corner of the building.

"What are you doing?"

"Figuring out how much open space you have." The woman stopped counting and shaded her eyes. "I'm finished. Are you ready to scale Mount Kilimanjaro?"

"It is a steep hill." Morgan grabbed the railing. "Have you ever climbed Mount Kilimanjaro?"

"Yeah, but it wasn't a big deal."

Morgan made a choking sound. "Climbing a mountain wasn't a big deal? I think it would be on the epic level."

"It's a freestanding mountain. Actually, it's the world's tallest freestanding mountain."

"What does that mean?"

"It stands alone and isn't part of a mountain range. Mount Kilimanjaro doesn't require skills or equipment...ropes, harnesses, ice axes, stuff like that. You hike or walk to the peak."

"You make it sound like a stroll in the park." Morgan wrinkled her nose. "Despite the lack of skill, you're still climbing a very tall mountain."

"True. Yeah. It was cool, but I doubt I'll do it again. Like I said..."

"You're ready to scale back on your adventurous endeavors," Morgan quipped.

Randi laughed. "Good one, and an accurate summary of my goals. I'm looking forward to slowing down. I've lost count of how many times I woke up in the morning and had no clue where I was."

"I don't think I would care for that, although I do like to travel...sometimes. Have you ever..." Morgan abruptly stopped, thinking her question might be a little too personal.

"Ever what?" Randi prompted.

"Don't mind me. I was going to ask what could be construed as a nosy question and, frankly, none of my business."

The woman waved dismissively. "I'm a pretty private person in a lot of ways, while in others, I'm an open book. If I don't like the question, I'll tell you to mind your own beeswax."

Morgan laughed out loud. "Your in-the-face honesty is refreshing."

"No sense in tiptoeing around. So, what's the question?"

"Have you ever been married?"

"Once. To a Japanese monk. It didn't last long."

Morgan's eyes grew round as saucers. "You married a monk?"

"No." Randi chuckled. "I'm joking. Although I read once Japanese monks are allowed to marry. I've never been married. I've had a few boyfriends, but they never panned out. It's hard to nurture a relationship when you're constantly traveling from place to place."

"That makes sense."

The women reached Locke Pointe's rear entrance, and Randi consulted her watch. "I have some notes and a few phone calls to make. What time are we heading over to Easton Estate?"

"Dinner is at seven sharp. Grandmother is a stickler for punctuality and..."

"And what?"

"She also has a dress code. No jeans, T-shirts, hats or casual wear at the dinner table."

"What about spandex?"

Morgan grimaced.

Randi made a slicing motion across her neck. "Spandex is out."

"I've never seen anyone show up for dinner wearing spandex."

"I'm kidding." Randi playfully punched her in the arm. "Gerard already warned me. I'll dress accordingly."

"Let's meet on the porch at six forty-five."

"You got it."

Morgan watched as Randi hustled down the long hall and hurried up the stairs. "Randi Colbane. You certainly are an interesting or, as Grandmother would say, a most *unusual* guest."

Chapter 9

Randi met her on the front porch at six forty-five on the dot wearing a pale blue dress with beaded trim and a denim jacket over the top. Morgan had no idea how her grandmother felt about denim, but the woman was wearing a dress, which meant she at least partially met her grandmother's attire requirements.

"Well?" Randi spun in a slow circle. "Does this meet your approval?"

"It's not my approval you have to meet. The dress is nice."

"Thanks. I haven't had one of these gems on in...well, probably a decade or more." Randi scratched her head and winced. "The wig is a little loose, so I'm trying to remind myself not to mess with it too much."

"It looks good."

"Lynn," Randi reminded her.

"Yes, we'll need to stick with the name Ms. Spade. Let's hit the road." During the drive, they passed Looking Glass Cottage and Morgan pointed it out.

Randi peered out the window, noting the lake directly across the street. "Cute cottage. You also have a sweet view."

"I do. Chester and I spend a lot of time walking along the shoreline."

"So would I." Randi shifted her gaze. "I'm curious. Why not move to Locke Pointe? Your cottage looks cozy and comfy, don't get me wrong, but it's not nearly as impressive as your other property."

"It's too much, too big for me. My roommate, Quinn, who also happens to be my best friend, and I are content living where we do. It has sentimental value and reminds me of my mother."

"Ah." Randi nodded knowingly. "I get it. If you ever change your mind, at least you have other options."

"Multiple other options."

They reached Easton Estate and Morgan parked off to the side, next to Quinn's car, before entering through the back.

Chester promptly trotted off to greet Mrs. Arnsby.

"There's my Chester." The cook grabbed a treat from the treat drawer and held it out. "Quinn is already here."

"Thanks. We parked next to her." Morgan licked her lips, eyeing the pies lined up on the counter. "I love lemon meringue pie."

"I hate to burst your bubble, but they're not lemon meringue pies. They're Canadian Prairies Province pies, also called flapper pies."

"They still look yummy."

"It's more of a custard than a tart lemon." Mrs. Arnsby had that look on her face, and Morgan suspected they were in for a history lesson about the pies. "A Prairies Province pie. It sounds intriguing."

"I wouldn't go as far as saying intriguing, but at least somewhat interesting. The recipe comes from Manitoba, to be precise." The cook told them the pies were popular back in the Roaring Twenties, which is where it picked up the "flapper" part of the name. "You won't see it served at too many restaurants these days. Once in a while I get a hankering to whip up a few, which is what I'll be serving for dessert this evening."

"They look delicious. Knowing your baking abilities, I'm sure they taste equally amazing."

"If you're trying to butter me up, it's working like a charm," Mrs. Arnsby turned to Randi, aka Lynn. "Hello."

"Where are my manners?" Morgan introduced her guest, this time as Lynn Spade.

The cook's brows furrowed. "Are you from around here?"

"I...uh. No, I'm not."

Morgan, suspecting Mrs. Arnsby sensed something was off, hurriedly wrapped up the introductions and propelled Lynn into the dining room. Brett, Quinn, Jax and Ben were already there, and she made another round of introductions.

Gerard and Elizabeth arrived moments later.

While Lynn chatted with the others, Morgan ran back into the kitchen to track down her pup.

Mrs. Arnsby caught Morgan's eye and hurried over. "I thought Richard, the man I met earlier, was coming to dinner."

"He...won't be. Lynn has taken his place," Morgan answered honestly.

"Something weird is going on," the cook muttered, a puzzled expression on her face.

"Weird like how?"

"It's a feeling. Lynn reminds me of Richard." The cook's jaw dropped. "They're related, aren't they?"

"In a roundabout way." Morgan patted her arm and turned to go.

"Perhaps you should start running background checks on guests." The woman trailed after Morgan, following her to the door.

"I'm pretty sure visitors aren't going to give me their social security numbers to book a stay."

"What about metal detectors? You could install metal detectors at all entry points."

"They're staying for relaxation, not to feel like they're going to prison." Morgan squeezed her arm. "I'll be all right. Lynn is harmless. I promise."

"If you say so."

"I do." Morgan thanked her for her concern and stepped into the hall.

Was Randi harmless? Yes.

Was she quirky? Most definitely...off the charts.

Chapter 10

Jax was the first to raise red flags during dinner, and to be honest, Morgan couldn't blame him. Inviting one of her bed-and-breakfast guests to Easton Estate for an evening meal with Grandmother and her friend, Gerard, would most assuredly raise a few eyebrows.

And if Mrs. Arnsby had shared her concerns about Richard, now Lynn, to Jax, who had a background in law enforcement, then he would undoubtedly zero in on their guest.

At least he waited until they were on the main course to engage her in conversation. "Ms. Spade, you're a guest staying at Locke Pointe Bed-and-Breakfast?"

"I am."

"Have you been to Easton Island before?"

"No. This is my first visit," Lynn replied.

"Are you enjoying your stay?"

"Immensely. I should have visited long ago."

"So, you've heard about Easton Island before?" Jax pressed. "Before booking your stay?"

"I have. Many times. I grew up in the Midwest."

"You found out about Locke Pointe and planned a visit?"

"I did. Although it's not just for pleasure. I'll be doing some work while I'm here."

Morgan, who had been taking a sip of water, began choking.

Lynn patted her on the back. "Are you okay?"

"Yeah," Morgan croaked. "I swallowed the wrong way."

Jax cast Morgan a concerned glance, but had no intention of being sidetracked. "What line of work are you in?"

Morgan held her breath while her guest contemplated his question.

"Investigations. Private investigations, to be specific, and my services are not cheap."

Jax drummed his fingers on the table, an intent look on his face. "You're working on a private investigation while you're here?"

"Correct."

"For Morgan?"

Elizabeth spoke up. "Jax, please do not interrogate our dinner guest. What Ms. Spade is doing here is none of our business unless it involves Morgan's safety and welfare."

"I can vouch for Lynn," Gerard added. "We've been friends for many years."

Gerard's assurance seemed to mollify Jax, and the conversation shifted to talk about Easton Island Airport with Gerard and Randi, singing its praises.

"Even with the emergency landing, the crew and staff on the ground did an excellent job of getting us off the plane quickly and safely."

"Which took more than a few years off my life," Elizabeth said.

Mrs. Arnsby directed the kitchen help to start removing empty dinner dishes. "I hope the meal was satisfactory."

"It was wonderful," Morgan said. "And healthy to boot. Grilled salmon, grilled asparagus, a tossed salad with fresh avocado slices."

"We're implementing some menu changes," Mrs. Arnsby explained. "Healthier, more plant-based meals. Except for the pie, which was a splurge."

"And that reminds me." Jax turned to Elizabeth. "The new treadmill has arrived. I can bring it up to your apartment in the morning whenever you're ready for it."

"Thank you, Jax. I promise to try to use it every day."

Ben looked as if he wanted to say something. It wasn't until after the meal ended that he pulled Elizabeth aside and they talked quietly in the corner.

Morgan, watching the exchange, sensed something was up. She caught Brett's eye and knew he felt the same. New dinner menus. A treadmill.

The siblings made their way across the room, catching the tail end of Elizabeth and Ben's conversation.

"...at the dock by two o'clock. I'll need an extra hour to make it to the mainland," Elizabeth said. "It took some finagling for the specialist to fit me in, so I don't want to miss this."

"I'll pick you up around front at one on the dot." Ben took a step back, inadvertently colliding with Brett, who was directly behind him.

"Brett...I uh...didn't see you standing there."

Morgan noticed her grandmother's shoulders tense. She slowly turned. "Morgan, Brett. What are you doing?"

"Wondering what's going on," Brett said.

Elizabeth's eyes flitted from one to the other. "What do you mean?"

"New and healthier dinner menus, a treadmill," Morgan said. "What specialist are you going to see?"

Ben began inching away. "I'll leave you to chat. Mrs. Arnsby looks like she could use some help." He hurried off.

"And Ben took off like the devil himself was chasing after him to avoid our conversation," Brett said.

"You have nothing to be concerned about." Elizabeth shrugged. "We can all stand to eat better and exercise more."

"And the specialist?" Morgan pressed. "What kind of specialist?"

"It's nothing to concern yourselves with. As much as I love both of you, I have no desire to discuss it."

Morgan could tell by the look on her grandmother's face the subject was closed. Something was afoot at Easton Estate and it was being kept from Brett and Morgan.

"As you wish." Brett forced a smile and followed the others into the library for after-dinner drinks.

Morgan checked on Chester, who was still in the kitchen, before joining the others in the library. She found Randi and Elizabeth standing off to the side. "I'm sorry if Jax came on a little strong."

"Came on a little strong? The dude is like a bulldog." Randi blew air through thinned lips. "I thought I was being interrogated by the FBI."

"Not the FBI, but close," Elizabeth said. "Jax is a former CSIS agent."

"Well, now I get it. He's very protective of Morgan."

"For good reason. Morgan's ex-husband stalked her, kidnapped, robbed and planned to kill her."

Randi's jaw dropped. "For real?"

"For real. I flew to Fort Myers recently to testify against him. He's currently in prison for peddling prescription drugs which didn't belong to him."

"He sounds like a real gem," Randi said sarcastically.

"You have no idea. Hence Jax's line of questioning. He considers it his job to protect me."

"Cool. I appreciate the clarification. I'll move him from the nosy jerk to an overzealous protective friend category."

"He is," Elizabeth replied. "But it doesn't mean he and the others aren't slightly suspicious about why you're here. If the medallion is authentic, it's only a matter of time before your cover is blown and my staff finds out exactly who you are."

"Which is why I'm using the private investigator story. It's my go-to cover. In a way, that's what I am. I investigate ancient artifacts." Randi placed both hands behind her back and began perusing the bookshelves. "You have an extensive library."

"It hardly ever gets used. Quinn and Morgan are the only two who use it."

She paused in front of the historical section. "I'm noticing a nice selection of Easton Island historical books."

"Any book published about the island is a part of my collection, along with several written about the Easton family."

"Very impressive," Randi said. "This island, Locke Pointe, Easton Estate. I have to admit, it's even better than I thought it would be."

"Has Morgan filled you in on the medallion's story?" Quinn asked.

"She has. It involved some clever sleuthing, putting all those pieces together and finding the secret hiding spot."

"Are you ready to inspect and authenticate the medallion?" Elizabeth asked.

"Ready whenever you are. I left my backpack in Morgan's SUV."

"I'll go grab it." With a furtive glance down the hall, Morgan slipped out the front door, making her way along the sidewalk to her vehicle.

The main garage's exterior and interior lights were on. Thankfully, Ben was nowhere in sight. She unlocked the passenger side door, grabbed Randi's backpack, and began backtracking toward the front.

"Morgan!"

She turned to find Jax waving her down and waited for him to catch up. "I was hoping I would catch you alone for a minute."

"What's up?"

"About dinner and your guest…"

"And your interrogation?" Morgan teased.

"I want to apologize if I came on too strong."

"I appreciate the apology, but there's no need. You're protective of me and for good reason, considering all Jason has put me through. Ran…Lynn is a unique person, an odd duck in some ways, but she's perfectly harmless. At least, I think she is."

"And she's a private investigator?" Jax asked. "Working for you?"

Morgan sucked in a breath. She could never lie to a man who had been nothing but kind, had saved her life and was loyal to a fault. For those reasons, along with so many others, she felt she needed to be straightforward, or at least as straightforward as she could, considering the circumstances.

"Lynn is here to help me. At least I hope she'll be able to help me. I know you're still on the fence about her and I don't blame you. Believe me, I don't. But please don't ask too many questions I can't answer right now."

Jax's expression softened, and their eyes met. "I only ask because I care."

"I know you do. I'm hoping that down the road, sometime soon, I can tell you what's going on, but not yet." Morgan bounced on the tips of her toes and gave him a quick hug. "Thank you for caring."

"You've assured me you're safe. That's all I need to know." Jax held his index and pinky fingers near his ear, as if making a call. "I'm only a phone call or text away."

"Duly noted." Morgan lifted Randi's backpack. "I better get going before the others think I got lost."

"What's in the bag?" Jax craned his neck. "Never mind. I'm sure I'll find out."

"Hopefully sooner rather than later." Morgan turned to go and stopped. "I don't want to put you on the spot, but is Grandmother all right?"

It was Jax's turn to look uncomfortable. "What do you mean?"

"Mrs. Arnsby implementing a new, healthier dinner menu. Grandmother buying a treadmill." Morgan told him she and Brett had overheard her talking to Ben about an appointment with a specialist.

"What did she say?" Jax asked.

"She got defensive and is refusing to talk about it."

"You, Elizabeth and Brett are like family."

"We are."

"Your grandmother is also my employer, which means I'm not at liberty to discuss her private business, even if you are related to her."

"In other words, you're not spilling the beans," Morgan said.

Jax didn't answer, but the look on his face told her what she was looking for. Elizabeth was seeing a specialist and wasn't willing to discuss it, which meant it could be something serious.

"I appreciate our chat." She held a finger to her lips. "Between the two of us. I'll get my answer even if I have to drag it out of her." Morgan excused herself and hurriedly darted back inside, catching up with the others who stood waiting for her in the hallway.

"We were beginning to wonder if you forgot about us," Elizabeth joked.

"Jax stopped me outside. He's still very...curious about Lynn."

"I suppose he is. We need to find out what we have as soon as possible. We can't keep this a secret forever." Elizabeth led the way down the long hall and into the office. Closing the door behind them, she walked over to the floor-to-ceiling shelves lining the back wall.

She slid a large self-portrait to the right, revealing a square black keypad.

Randi let out a low whistle. "I'm digging this house's James Bond-ish vibe."

"It's more than a secret keypad," Morgan said.

"Please look away while I enter the code."

The others turned while Elizabeth entered the code. The wall moved, and the estate's hidden room appeared.

"This is Easton Estate's panic room," Elizabeth explained. "The room is waterproof, flood proof, bombproof and earthquake proof. Fresh air is piped in to keep it an even ambient temperature." She stepped inside the dimly lit room, returning a short time later carrying the medallion's box. She set it on the desk and gently lifted the lid.

Randi inched closer. "Will you look at that?"

The others stood by quietly, watching as the archaeologist removed a pair of gloves from her backpack and slipped them on. Next, she slid a pair of reading glasses on and held the medallion toward the light. "It's in incredible condition. The box protected it from the elements. If it hadn't been kept preserved, it wouldn't look half as pretty."

Morgan noticed the woman's hand trembled as she reached inside her bag again, this time removing what resembled a walkie-talkie. She fiddled with the buttons before pressing the tip against the medallion's surface. "What is that?"

"An ultrasonic testing device. I'm testing the composition of the coin." Randi went into a long spiel about how different coins produced distinct echoes. Meanwhile, the handheld machine spit out a thin stream of paper. It reminded Morgan of a gas pump receipt.

She finished testing the top and flipped the medallion over. The second round of testing produced an equally long paper trail.

After finishing, she carefully tore the printout off, slid the device back in her bag and removed a heavy-duty flashlight. "So far, so good. It appears to be authentic. The Shifting Sands Medallion contains specific markings, certain traces produced when the artifact was created." Randi began mumbling under her breath while Morgan held hers.

Finally, she placed the medallion back inside the box, turned the flashlight off, and removed her reading glasses.

"Well?" Elizabeth asked. "What is your professional opinion?"

"I have some good news and some bad news."

Chapter 11

Morgan said the first thing that popped into her head after the archaeologist's announcement. "Give us the good news first."

"I believe the medallion is authentic. In fact, I'm almost one hundred percent certain it is."

"What's the bad news?" Brett asked.

Randi waved the trail of paper in the air. "I need to send this to a lab in California to verify the machine's results and to get a second opinion. Nothing in the archaeological world is accepted without a second opinion."

Morgan's heart plummeted. "How long will it take?"

"For a verbal or to have the actual certification in your hot little hands?"

"Both."

"I'll upload the results, along with photographs and other information, tonight. With any luck, my colleague will have time to go over them tomorrow. Worst-case scenario is forty-eight hours, give or take a day."

"And the certificate? How long before we have that?" Elizabeth asked.

"I can print out a copy, but the original with the raised gold seal will take a few days to get here." Randi lifted a hand. "We need to discuss one minor detail. The fee."

"The fee?"

"For both phases of the authentication. I have expenses and will need to be reimbursed for my time."

"Yes, of course," Morgan said. "Gerard forwarded a ballpark figure to me. As soon as I have the total for your time, the lab and your colleague's time, plus the certificate, I'll write you a check."

"Perfect." Randi removed her gloves and tossed them in her backpack. "I would be happy to stick around for a few days until the certificate arrives. Depending on how quickly the story leaks out, I might even be able to help you handle the press."

"The press," Quinn repeated.

"News media. As soon as the results are authenticated, the information is uploaded into a national database, accessible by archaeologists who follow the finds."

"You're saying as soon as you and your colleague verify the medallion is legit, and the certificate is in the mail, hundreds of other people will also find out."

"In a nutshell," Randi confirmed. "Which could be exciting or...not so much, depending on how you look at it."

"We're about to be overrun," Elizabeth muttered. "Is there any chance you can ask your colleague to confirm authentication and hold off on entering the results in the database?"

"I'm sending it to Newt. He's discreet. If I ask him to hold off, he'll keep it under wraps for a few days, although it probably won't matter." Randi stated several other archaeologists and associates worked at the facility, which meant keeping it a secret for any length of time would be nearly impossible. "The bottom line is as soon as I send the file to him, the clock is ticking."

"We understand," Elizabeth said. "Do you mind if I have a private word with Morgan?"

"Not at all." Gerard placed a light hand on Randi's back and whisked her out of the office, with Brett and Quinn trailing behind.

Elizabeth waited until they were gone. "Randi has confirmed what we believed all along."

Morgan plucked the medallion from the box. "I had hoped for more time to decide what to do with it."

"Me too. Unfortunately, as she pointed out, we won't have long."

"And Easton Island will be overrun." Morgan pressed the ancient artifact between her palms, feeling both its weight and warmth. "I would like to figure out the next step before that happens."

"Which will depend on who the medallion belongs to," Elizabeth pointed out. "We need her opinion on who the rightful owner or owners are."

"I'm almost certain it isn't me." Morgan briefly closed her eyes.

"Are you all right, dear? I thought you would be pleased."

"I am, but I'm also worried about who might show up looking for it."

"And you're concerned about Easton Estate being named as the location once rumors start circulating," Elizabeth guessed.

"Yes."

"Unless they don't know where it is, although it wouldn't be too difficult to figure out if it was at one of your properties or here."

"Making Easton Estate, Looking Glass Cottage and Locke Pointe all targets." Morgan flipped it over, absentmindedly running her thumb over the top. "Maybe I should lock it up in the bank's vault."

Elizabeth pursed her lips.

"You don't like the idea."

"No. Something tells me once the story of the medallion resurfacing after all of these years goes public, not only will certain private individuals become interested in it, but also government officials."

Morgan blinked rapidly. "Government officials with a unique twist."

"On both the Canadian and American side," Elizabeth said. "We need to keep the medallion close at hand, but it doesn't mean we can't send them on a wild goose chase."

"Leading everyone to believe we've moved it to a different location?"

"Precisely." Elizabeth snapped her fingers. "We may have to enlist the help of Wyatt and that nice Officer Grady MacDonald to make a big show that it's being securely transported away from Easton Island."

"I like the way you're thinking. For now, let's keep the ball rolling." Morgan hurried to the door and summoned the others back inside. "Grandmother and I are ready."

"To pull the trigger?" Randi asked.

"Yes. We're also considering moving the medallion off the island to another secure location."

"That might not be a bad idea," Gerard said. "Make sure you let the press people and public know it's no longer here. Are you thinking about moving it to Toronto?"

"It's an option," Elizabeth said. "We also have a few connections on the East Coast, individuals who might be able to assist us."

Randi began packing up her tools. "This is the most exciting find since...well, the Great Lakes discovery a couple of months ago."

Morgan watched her tuck the printouts into the side pocket of her bag. "Is the Great Lakes find still hush-hush?"

"For the most part." Randi glanced over her shoulder, toward the door. "You've heard of Nessie."

"The Loch Ness monster," Elizabeth said.

"Yeah. This find makes Nessie look like a Microraptor, one of the smallest dinosaur fossil specimens ever found." Randi zipped her backpack shut. "The exploration is ongoing. We're still not sure if we'll be able to bring this thing to the surface."

"Meaning it might empty the lake?" Brett joked.

"It's a monster. I'll give you that." Randi extended a hand to Elizabeth. "If, for some reason, I don't see you again, thank you for your hospitality, for dinner and for allowing me to assist in the authentication."

"My pleasure. Safe travels, wherever you end up next." While Elizabeth placed the medallion back inside the safe, Gerard accompanied the others to the front.

"I'll walk Quinn to her car," Brett said.

"And you'll be home…" Quinn tapped Morgan's arm.

"Later." Morgan made googly eyes at Quinn when the others weren't looking. "At least a couple hours from now if you want to entertain or have company over."

"Very funny." Her best friend slugged her in the arm, shooting her a warning look.

Brett, oblivious to the women's playful banter, casually glanced toward the front of the house. "I'm sure Grandmother and Gerard could use some time alone, which means it might not be a bad idea for me to find something else to do for a few hours," he hinted.

"I don't want you to feel unwelcome in your own home," Gerard protested.

Brett's expression grew mischievous. "I'm sensing you don't want to be alone with my grandmother. Fair enough. I'll set up a game of chess in the library. We can stay up until the wee hours of the morning."

"I...uh." Gerard, realizing Brett was teasing him, smiled. "I suppose a few hours in front of the fireplace with a lovely woman such as Elizabeth would be a splendid way to end the evening."

"It will be much more enjoyable than spending it with me." Brett patted his arm. "I'll make myself scarce."

"Hang out with Quinn," Morgan offered. "I'm sure she won't mind."

Behind Brett's back, Quinn shot daggers at her friend. When she spun back around, she was all smiles. "You're welcome to come over. We don't want to get in the way of a budding romance."

"For everyone involved," Morgan muttered under her breath.

Quinn elbowed her, the smile never leaving her face. "I could use an evening stroll to burn off some of Mrs. Arnsby's delicious pie."

"It's a date...deal," Brett said. "I'll grab my jacket and follow you home."

Quinn waited until he was gone. She wagged her finger. "Stop playing matchmaker."

"Why? Brett was hinting around." Morgan smiled slyly. "I was giving him a helping hand. Grandmother and Gerard could use a little privacy. I see this as a win-win for everyone."

"It looks like love is in the air. We'll see you around, Gerard." Randi slung her backpack over her shoulder and hugged the man. "Keep in touch."

"Same to you." Gerard gave her a light kiss on the cheek. "It wouldn't hurt for you to come home for the holidays once in a while."

"You know how I am about those family get-togethers." Randi rolled her eyes. "Aunt Edna sniping at Uncle Leo. Cousin Dean is always trying to sell me life insurance."

"But that's what families are for—to annoy one another."

"I'll think about it. I've got a few months to figure out what I'll do during the holidays."

"You two are..." Morgan struggled to follow the conversation.

"Randi is my niece," Gerard said. "She asked me to keep our relationship on the...how do you say it?"

"Down low," Morgan suggested.

"Yep, and now that I've gotten to know you, I figured it was safe to let the cat out of the bag."

Randi gave her uncle one last hug. "I'll let you know what happens with the medallion. With any luck, I'll hear back soon. You'll still be here, and I can share the good news with everyone."

"I hope so." Gerard told them goodbye and returned inside.

Morgan waited for Brett and Quinn to leave first before she and Randi made their way to her vehicle and climbed in. "I had no idea you and Gerard were related. Does my grandmother know?"

"Yeah. Uncle G told her earlier today."

"The whole spiel about not meeting with strangers even if a friend arranged it was a cover?"

"Sort of. I was still on the fence until I met you in person, even though my uncle vouched for you. He isn't one to do a lot of favors for people and believe me, he gets asked often."

"But he did it for Grandmother because of their relationship."

"Uncle G digs her."

"I would say the feeling is mutual," Morgan said.

"I'm talking romantically. He's been lonely since my aunt passed away. The only woman I've ever heard him mention is your grandmother, which is another reason why I agreed to meet both of you."

"Because you were curious."

"Bingo. She's a sweet lady, but like I said..."

"She can be intimidating." Morgan finished her sentence.

"So now you've heard my story." Randi patted her bag. "I'll send my findings over to Newt as soon as I get back to my room and ask him to keep it on the down low."

"I would appreciate it." Morgan cast the woman a side glance. "There is one thing that has been on my mind from the moment I found the medallion."

"What to do with it if it's legit?"

"Yes. If there is a rightful owner, I want to return it to him...to them."

"Which is what I've been working on, to trace the origins." Randi told her she had access to several research sites she was using to help her obtain the background information needed, including tracing the medallion all the way back to its creation.

"How much do you think it's worth?"

"It's hard to say. It could be millions, potentially even priceless," Randi said. "Considering the level of interest over the years and the history, I would guess on the higher end."

Morgan tightened her grip on the steering wheel, her mind reeling. Millions, possibly priceless. Today's news meant they were embarking on an exciting, yet potentially dangerous, journey.

And, as of tonight, the clock was ticking.

Chapter 12

Randi grew quiet as they pulled into Locke Pointe's driveway, her expression thoughtful when they made their way up the steps. It was clear there was something on the woman's mind.

"Are you having second thoughts about the medallion?"

"No. I'm almost certain it's the real deal."

"You remembered something and need to leave sooner than originally planned?"

"I have a few more days. This place is exactly what I've been looking for." The woman rubbed the sides of her arms. "Although I have to admit, I've been getting weird vibes."

"Weird vibes," Morgan repeated. "Good or bad?"

"Restless. Like restless vibes, if that makes sense."

"You're getting restless, weird vibes about my place?" Morgan bit her lower lip. She'd had many feelings, many emotions about Locke Pointe, but all of them positive...how the home had been a happy place, full of loving memories.

"Not necessarily Locke Pointe, but in this area." Randi rolled her shoulders. "It's gone. I'll see you in the morning?"

Morgan reminded her about the breakfast hours and parted ways with her guest near the stairs. She and Chester meandered into the kitchen, where Tina was prepping for the following morning's breakfast.

"I thought I passed Greg's car on the way here. Did he just leave?"

"Yeah. He was working late."

"Was there a problem?"

"I'm not sure," the cook confessed. "He and Ronni were in the office talking before he left. I believe she's still here."

"Good. I'll find out from her what's going on."

Tina placed the breakfast bakes in the refrigerator and untied her apron. "I'm heading out. I'll see you in the morning."

"See you then." Morgan locked the rear entrance door behind her before trekking to the office.

"Knock. Knock." She peeked around the corner and found Ronni seated at the desk.

"Hey, Morgan. How was dinner at the estate?"

Morgan gave her a thumbs up. "Very nice. As usual, Mrs. Arnsby outdid herself."

"Jane is a gem." Ronni leaned back in her chair. "I was going over our reservations. July is almost booked solid."

"Business is going even better than I thought it would. Have I thanked you lately for offering to help me with this place?" Morgan sank into the chair opposite her.

"Multiple times. I'm thoroughly enjoying my new role, meeting the guests and hearing their stories, how much they love staying here. It makes it all worthwhile."

"Running a small B&B is a whole different ballgame than working for Corporate America."

"And better in so many ways," Ronni said. "Now I know what people mean when they say they love their chosen career. They don't consider it to be a job."

"I'm glad you're enjoying it." Morgan leaned forward, placing her hands on her knees. "If it ever gets to be too much, please let me know."

"I will, but with only twelve guests max, I don't see how I could ever become overwhelmed, not to mention you have a great team in place. Tina, the room attendants. Greg does an excellent job of maintaining the grounds. He's very conscientious about making sure he picks the guests up on time and never complains about carrying their luggage to their rooms."

"He was working late tonight," Morgan said. "Was there a problem?"

"No. He asked earlier if he could put some extra hours in. He's trying to stash away some extra cash."

"He doesn't think he's making enough?"

"Greg is trying to save money to move out," Ronni said.

Morgan had learned some time ago from Ben Baker, Greg's uncle, who was also Easton Estate's chauffeur, that he lived with his mother above Easton Harbor Art Gallery. Her grandmother rented the place to them at a fraction of the going rate to help the family, who had limited sources of income.

"Move out of the apartment he and his mother share?"

Ronni nodded. "Thanks to you, he's found a job he loves, one that works well for him and he has an eye on the future."

Morgan popped out of the chair. She wandered to the window, her eyes drawn to the carriage house out back. "We're not using the carriage house for anything more than storage."

"True."

Morgan spun around, her mind whirling. "What if I renovated it?"

"And offered to let Greg live there?" Ronni folded her hands. "I think it's an excellent idea. It would be helpful to have an employee, a staff member, living on the premises."

"In the event guests need something." Morgan warmed to the idea. "I like it. A lot. In fact, I think I'll head out there tonight to snap a few pictures and send them to my construction guy to see what he thinks."

"Before you go." Ronni stopped her, handing her a handful of expenditures needing approval.

"You're so good about staying on top of the bills." Morgan ran her hand over her head. "Sometimes I wonder if I bit off more than I can chew. There's a lot more to this B&B business than I thought."

"Which is true of any business. You have a better handle on it than you think you do." After finishing, Ronni placed the papers inside the file folder. "I didn't mean to hold you up. Are you going to wait until tomorrow to check out the carriage house?"

"No. I would rather do it tonight, so I can get those pictures over to my construction guy, Steve. I don't want to mention it to Greg or get his hopes up until I find out what can be done."

"I don't blame you." Ronni shut her laptop and stood. "Something tells me he'll be thrilled."

"Me too." Morgan caught up with her at the door and glanced at her phone. "There are no texts from guests needing anything."

"No news is good news," Ronni quipped. "If you don't mind, I'll tag along while you scope out the potential apartment."

"Not at all. I can always use a second set of eyes. You might notice something I overlook." Morgan grabbed her purse. She turned the lights down and then checked to make sure the exterior doors were locked before following Ronni and her pup out onto the porch.

Chester scrambled down the steps and stopped to investigate several new plantings alongside his favorite tree. He obediently caught up when Morgan called him to her side.

It took a few tries before she finally found the carriage house key. "I need to have Joyce from Locke and Key come over here one of these days to re-key a few of these locks."

She opened the door and flipped the lights on, illuminating the spacious interior. On one side was a lawnmower and edge trimmer, a workbench and toolbox, along with several bags of mulch and lawn fertilizer, all neatly organized by Greg.

The women circled the perimeter before climbing a set of steep steps leading to the second floor loft. Morgan critically eyed the space. "The ceilings up here are too low. I think sectioning off part of the main level would work better."

"I agree." Ronni carefully backed down the steps. "The good news is there is already electric and plumbing in place."

"You're right." Morgan had completely forgotten about the half bath tucked away in the corner. "I'm starting to think this is doable." She snapped several pictures of the wiring, the electrical box, the bathroom, floors, and windows.

After finishing, she tapped out a text to her construction guy, attached the pictures and hit the send button. "Steve was able to schedule repairs to the main house pretty quickly. Hopefully, he'll have time to squeeze this project in."

Despite the late hour, Morgan received a prompt reply, confirming he had read her email and promised to take a look at what she'd sent the following morning. He also asked if it would be possible to swing by and see it in person.

With a few back-and-forth messages, he arranged to stop by the next day. "Remind me to unlock the side door in the morning, in case I'm not around when Steve gets here."

Backtracking, the women exited through the side door. Morgan flipped the lights off and twisted the doorknob, making sure it was locked. "Where's Chester?"

"I don't know," Ronni said. "He must've sneaked out."

Morgan began calling her pup.

Woof. Chester's bark echoed from the direction of the path leading down to the beach.

"Chester Charleston Easton!" Morgan scolded. "Get back here!"

"It sounds like he found something," Ronni said.

Morgan glimpsed him near the top of the hill, his attention focused on the beach area at the bottom.

A burst of bright light flashed across the side of the kayak and canoe storage building and then disappeared.

The hair on the back of Morgan's neck stood straight up. "Someone is down by the lake."

Chapter 13

"We need to run back to the house and find some sort of weapon."

"Like a gun?" Morgan reached into her purse, opened her carrying case, and pulled out her gun.

Ronni's jaw dropped. "You're carrying a gun around?"

"I have ever since Jason kidnapped me."

"Can't say that I blame you. Maybe we should call Wyatt to see if he's in the area."

Wyatt, who also happened to be a Locke Village police officer, was working, and she knew he would be there as soon as she called. "I don't want to jump the gun until we can figure out what's going on."

"Jump the gun? Cute pun," Ronni teased. "True. It could be one of your guests taking an evening stroll."

The women crept across the yard, catching up with Chester, who was still laser-focused on the lights bouncing off the shoreline and near the water's edge. Moving stealthily, they crept down the hill, with the pup close by their side.

Morgan released the safety on her gun and adjusted her grip. The light shifted, bouncing off the side of the storage building again. Moving yet closer, she could hear voices. Actually, it was only one voice.

"Lynn?" Morgan called out her guest's name, reminding herself Ronni wasn't "in the loop" about the medallion and the reason for Randi's visit.

A shadowy figure stepped into the light. "Morgan?"

Morgan relaxed her stance. "What are you doing?"

"Setting up camp." Lynn motioned to a partially assembled dome tent. "Am I bothering you?"

"No, but you alerted Chester, so we came down here to see what was going on."

"Carrying a handgun? I thought Easton Island was a modern-day version of Mayberry," the woman joked.

"Close, but not quite." Morgan slid the safety in place and put it back in the carry case. "Thanks to my ex-husband's actions, I carry a gun."

"This looks like more than a one-woman operation. Would you like some help?" Ronni asked.

"If you don't mind." Lynn grabbed a pole. "I'm kicking myself for not setting up camp while it was still daylight."

Morgan made her way around to the other side. "Is there a problem with your room?"

"No, it's great." Lynn confessed she sometimes had trouble sleeping and felt more comfortable out in the open air. "The swankier the digs, the harder it is for me to relax."

"What do you do for a living, if you don't mind me asking?" Ronni asked.

"I research interesting stuff."

"Which involves spending a lot of time outdoors?"

Morgan could see Ronni was struggling to figure out what the woman meant, and quickly changed the conversation. "You should be careful walking along the shoreline at night."

"I wasn't planning on exploring," Lynn said. "But I heard this unusual sound."

"Like what?"

"Whoooo...hooo...wee...woo."

Morgan repeated the sound. "Maybe it was the wind rustling through the trees."

"I thought that at first, but it wasn't coming from the woods. Although it could have been an owl."

"Did you see anyone?"

"No."

"We'll check it out as soon as we finish setting up."

The trio made quick work of assembling the small tent. After finishing, Randi placed a sleeping bag inside and propped her backpack next to the door.

"Is this what was in the heavy bag you checked at the airport?" Morgan asked. "You travel with a tent?"

"Yeah. I've learned over the years I end up needing it about half the time."

Ronni stepped on one of the anchors, pressing it deeper into the sandy soil. "Do you camp out in hotel parking lots?"

"I have and let me tell you that you can hear some very interesting conversations." Lynn pulled out a spotlight and turned it on. "I could've sworn there was something out there."

"The Lilac Inn next door is haunted," Ronni said. "You may have encountered Grace Coates."

"Haunted?" Lynn let out a whoop. "I love spooky stuff. Have you seen the ghost?"

"No, but several guests claim to have seen her."

"Cool beans. This place is getting better by the minute."

"You'll need to make sure you're not blocking access to the canoes and kayaks tomorrow morning," Morgan said.

"No worries. I'm an early riser. I'll take the tent down before the first ray of sunlight peeks over the horizon." Lynn turned the light off and tiptoed back to her tent. "Thanks for helping me set up."

"You're welcome. We'll let you get some rest." Morgan called her pup and turned to go. "Do you need help with anything else?"

"Nope. I'm all set. Are you heading home?"

"Yes. Ronni and I are leaving." Morgan patted her purse. "I have my cell phone with me in case you need to text or call."

"I'll be fine." Lynn stifled a yawn. "Oh, by the way. Remember when I asked for the internet login to send information to my colleague out in California?"

"I do."

"It's done." Lynn made a circle with her thumb and index finger. "Sent and received."

"I'm glad...the internet didn't give you any problems, and you took care of what you needed to. Thank you for the update," Morgan said. "See you in the morning."

Ronni waited until they were out of earshot and at the top of the hill. "She's a very unusual woman."

"Unusual, eccentric," Morgan said. "What do you think she saw and heard?"

"Who knows?" Ronni shrugged. "Could be nothing. It could be she has a very vivid imagination."

They reached the parking lot and Morgan waited for Ronni to drive off before slowly following behind. Had Lynn heard and glimpsed something hovering over the lake? True, she was an unusual person, but from what little she knew about the woman, she wasn't easily spooked or prone to making things up.

*****

Morgan reached the cottage and found Quinn's car was the only one parked in the driveway. She let herself in and immediately noticed the fragrant aroma of orange blossoms, her friend's favorite scent.

She dropped her purse on the counter and strolled into the living room where Quinn was cozied up on the couch, her laptop by her side and a candle burning brightly on top of their coffee table. "Hey, Morgan."

"Hey, Quinn. Brett left already?"

"A few minutes ago. We made marshmallow cereal treats. There are a bunch in the fridge if you're hungry."

"Thanks." Morgan eased onto the other end of the couch. She grabbed a pillow and tucked it against her chest. "I didn't get a chance to ask him, but will he be home for a while this time?"

"Yeah. He'll be hanging around for a few more days." Quinn shot her a quick glance. "I thought you two kept an online schedule."

"We do, but I don't check it every day. Brett texts or calls if he needs something." Morgan changed the subject. "Are we still on for our girl's trip to the city?"

"You betcha. I think I already mentioned he reserved a private booth for The Phantom of the Opera."

"You did. It will be fun. I'm looking forward to it."

"The three amigas...you, me and Grace."

Morgan leaned her head back and closed her eyes.

"Are you okay?" Quinn gently nudged her with her foot.

"It's been a long day. I have a lot on my mind...Randi's arrival, finding out about the medallion."

From the moment the archaeologist had confirmed its authenticity, Morgan couldn't stop thinking about it. What if her additional research gave no clear indication about who the rightful owner was? What would Morgan do with it? Donate it to a museum? If so, which one?

"It could be a big deal, a major deal," Quinn said. "Major enough to rewrite history books."

"It could," Morgan agreed. "Randi sent it to her colleague in California. We should have confirmation in the next day or so and then the real fun begins."

"You'll figure it out," Quinn said confidently. "You always have. How we're going to keep people from beating down our door looking for the medallion or a story might be a little trickier."

"Easton Estate is protected. Unfortunately, our cozy little cottage is a completely different story."

"I noticed your grandmother and Gerard giving each other the look." Quinn winked. "Love is in the air."

"As long as she's happy. To me, her happiness is all that matters."

The friends chatted for a few more minutes until Wyatt called to check in. "I'm going to take this call from Wyatt and turn in. Don't forget to put the candle out before heading to bed."

Quinn promptly blew it out and closed her laptop. "I think I'll turn in too. See you in the morning. Tell him I said hello."

"Will do." Morgan answered the call on her way to the porch to let Chester out. "Hey, Wyatt."

"Hey, beautiful. How did it go? Did you get your answer on the medallion?"

"Yes. Lynn err...Randi is certain it's authentic." Morgan filled him in on what had transpired before summing it up. "Now, we wait for the final word from Randi's colleague. As soon as we have confirmation and he enters the results into the archaeologist's national database, we'll need to move fast."

"You'll need twenty-four-hour bodyguards."

"Or to throw everyone off by leading them to believe it's no longer on Easton Island." Morgan told him what she and her grandmother had discussed.

"In other words, you make a big deal about it being moved off the island."

"Maybe. Unless we can come up with a better idea."

"How is your guest? You mentioned before she was a little odd."

"Definitely odd. I put her up in the Somewhere in Time suite. Instead of sleeping in her room, she pitched a tent down by the beach."

"Wow. Well, maybe that's what she's used to. Rugged living."

Morgan told him about her hearing noises and seeing something out in the water. "I think she believes she saw and heard something."

"Charlotte Coates' ghost?"

"Could be. Or maybe it was an owl. I hope she's okay staying out there alone."

"You said she's traveled all over the world to some dangerous places," Wyatt said.

"She has."

"Then a couple nights along the Lake Huron shoreline should be safe." Wyatt's voice faded. "Hey, I gotta take this last call."

"I'll let you go. Love you."

"Love you too. Don't worry about the other. We'll figure it out."

Morgan ended the call and ushered her pup back inside the house.

She locked up and trailed behind him, making a beeline for her bathroom. In some respects, life on Easton Island had become an easy ebb and flow. Each day was a little different, with new guests arriving and others leaving.

Ronni was a blessing, helping Morgan navigate the ins and outs of B&B ownership. She thought about Greg and what a hard worker he was. She couldn't blame him for wanting a place of his own. If Steve thought he could convert a portion of the carriage house to usable living space at a reasonable price, Morgan would move forward with the plan.

She made a mental note to follow up with him the next morning to pin him down on a timeline.

Morgan finished getting ready and climbed into bed. She tucked the covers under her chin and waited for Chester to pick his spot. "Well, buddy. It looks like there are budding romances between Quinn and Brett, not to mention Grandmother and Gerard. What do you think about that?"

The pup licked her hand and flopped over into his favorite position, resting his paw on her arm.

Morgan absentmindedly scratched his head and began mulling over the evening meal at Easton Estate.

It was clear the staff was concerned about Elizabeth's health and working with her to make significant changes. Seeing a specialist could mean any number of things. Adding to the fact she was cleaning out her apartment, parting with treasured mementos and the warning signs were piling up. Something was clearly happening.

Morgan couldn't bear the thought of losing the one person who had loved her unconditionally, been by her side, her champion and staunchest supporter during her darkest days.

She clenched her jaw, fighting the urge to burst into tears. Despite her resolve, a lone tear leaked out of the corner of her eye and down the side of her face.

Chester, sensing her sadness, snuggled closer, trying to comfort Morgan. "I can't bear the thought of losing Grandmother. Just as soon as she's ready to talk about what's going on, I'm going to do whatever it takes to help make sure she's around to see those great-grandchildren she keeps talking about."

Morgan prayed for her grandmother and was filled with a sense of peace. God wouldn't take away the one person who mattered most to her. He just wouldn't.

Chapter 14

Morgan, bleary-eyed from tossing and turning half the night, worrying about her grandmother's health, stifled a yawn as she studied the handwritten estimate Steve, her contractor, had given her. "This is in line with what I expected. How long do you think it will take?"

"I can squeeze the carriage house in between my other jobs, if you don't mind giving me a somewhat flexible schedule," Steve said. "If there aren't any major issues, I believe I can knock out adding wiring, extra outlets, additional pipes and plumbing, the framing and drywall in eight weeks."

"I'm fine with you fitting me in." Morgan held up a spare key. "Here's a key. Email me the final figures. I'll sign off and get the deposit over."

"Thanks for the work. I'll do the best I can." Steve slipped the key into his pocket. "Are you adding an additional guest space out here?"

"I'm going to offer to rent it to Greg Baker, my new handyman and groundskeeper. If he doesn't want it, Plan B will be to turn it into an additional suite."

"Greg Baker, as in Ben Baker's nephew?" Steve asked.

"Yes. You know Greg?"

"I sure do. He's a good guy. I've hired him for a few odd jobs here and there. It's hard finding good, steady year-round employment on the island."

"I'm happy to have him. He's looking for a place to live."

"Have you ever been inside the apartment he shares with his mother?"

"No, but I've heard it's small."

"Your grandmother rents it at a low monthly rate because money is tight, but I have to say if I was Greg, I would be ready to find a new place too, especially if I could afford it." Her contractor promised to have the paperwork over shortly.

After he left, Morgan tracked Greg down and found him tightening the mailbox's hinges.

"Morning, Morgan."

"Good morning. I've been meaning to mention that the mailbox needed some attention."

"Ronni told me the door kept flopping open and asked me to take a look at it." He tested the door. "It's as good as new."

"Thank you." Morgan tilted her head toward the flowerbeds lining both sides of the walkway leading to the front porch. "The gardens and flowers are thriving under your careful care."

He offered her a shy smile. "I never realized how green my thumb was."

"You've put in a lot of hard work around here and it shows." Morgan changed the subject. "Do you have a minute?"

"Sure." Greg's smile vanished. "Is there a problem?"

"No. Not a problem. Ronni mentioned that you're trying to save money to move out of the apartment you and your mom share."

"I am. I hope it's okay."

"A little overtime won't break the bank, although I might have a solution." Morgan and Greg crossed the yard and stepped into the carriage house. "If I converted a portion of this into an apartment, would you be interested in renting it from me?"

Greg's eyes lit. "Seriously?"

"My contractor has already stopped by. He told me he could have it ready to go in roughly two months, toward the end of summer."

"It's hard to find a place to rent on the island and whatever is out there is out of my price range. How much were you thinking?"

Morgan rattled off a reasonable monthly rental fee.

"Yes, ma'am. I would most definitely be interested."

"Good. Steve is going to squeeze the renovation into his schedule." Morgan told Greg she'd already given him a key. "It won't be large," she warned. "But it will have a separate bedroom, a kitchen, a living room, dining area and a full bath."

Greg grabbed her hand and shook it so hard her head wobbled. "Thank you, Morgan. You have no idea how much this means to me. As much as I love my mom, we're crammed in our apartment like sardines."

"I'm happy I can help. As soon as it's ready, I'll draw up a rental agreement."

Greg thanked her again, and the smile never left his face as he walked off.

"God, you sure know how to work small miracles every day," Morgan whispered under her breath. "Keep them coming."

Breakfast was almost over by the time she slipped back inside. She helped Tina and the cleaning staff finish clearing the tables and then sampled some leftovers, a generous piece of the breakfast bake along with crispy slices of bacon tucked inside a buttery croissant that nearly melted in her mouth.

"I noticed your construction guy was here earlier," Tina said. "Are you adding more guest rooms to the carriage house?"

"I'm putting in a small apartment for Greg."

"He's a good, hard worker," she said. "And been through some rough times."

Morgan remembered Jax telling her how Captain Davey had let him go because he couldn't keep up. As opposed to the bustling harbor, working at Locke Pointe was at a much slower pace, one which allowed the man to flourish. His moving in would be a win-win for everyone, and she couldn't wait to hand Greg the keys.

The morning passed quickly. She and Ronni met to go over the upcoming guests' arrival and departure schedules before her manager excused herself to run some errands.

Meanwhile, Morgan and Chester meandered around, finally making their way down to the beach area. The only remnants of Randi's campsite were a few small holes where they'd driven spikes into the ground to secure her tent.

Chester trotted off to investigate a chunk of driftwood and Morgan trailed behind, thinking about what Randi had said, how she'd heard noises and glimpsed something out in the water.

If she had been in the woman's shoes, she would have promptly packed up her tent and returned to her room. Although in her line of work, odd occurrences and spooky sightings were probably the norm.

Morgan shuddered at the thought of sleeping alongside ancient ruins, rumored to be haunted, thousands of years old and once the stomping grounds of world leaders, the scene of bloody battles and who knew what else.

Ting.

Morgan's cell phone chimed. It was Quinn. *Hey. I'm up front dropping off some mail that was delivered to our place instead of Locke Pointe. Where are you?*

Down by the water. I'm on my way.

"C'mon, Chester." Morgan called her pup. They returned to the main house to find not only Quinn waiting for them but also two women, in their late twenties, if she had to guess.

"These two are looking for a place to stay," Quinn said.

"My sister and I have been staying at the Lilac Inn next door."

"Grace's place?" Morgan clarified.

"Yes. We were wondering if you had any rooms available."

"I believe so. Let me check." Morgan slipped inside and stepped behind the check-in desk. "When were you thinking?"

"We're looking for a room for tonight through the weekend."

Morgan's head shot up. "You're checking out of the Lilac Inn early?"

The popular inn next door was booked solid from Memorial Day through Labor Day. In fact, time after time, she'd greeted guests who had tried to book rooms there only to discover they were sold out. Several of them had even told her that Grace suggested they call Morgan to inquire about availability.

The fact someone was checking out of there and into Locke Pointe was new to Morgan. Grace's inn was wonderful. Her breakfasts were topnotch. The suites were all elegantly appointed.

Upon stepping through the front door, visitors were immediately greeted like family, with cozy comfort enveloping all who entered. In fact, Morgan tried hard to emulate her friend's success, soaking up all the knowledge and tips Grace had so generously shared.

"We are." One woman confided they had booked a five-night stay at the inn but had only been there one night. "It came so highly rated and reviewed."

"Was there a problem with the room or the food?" Morgan needed to know why the sisters had checked out so she could give Grace a heads up.

"No. The room was perfect. We had a fabulous view overlooking Lake Huron."

"Our evening reception was fun. We met some interesting people and breakfast this morning?"

The second sister patted her stomach. "Was divine. I'm stuffed."

"So, what was the problem?"

They exchanged an uneasy glance.

"You're going to think we're crazy."

"I won't. I promise." Morgan crossed her arms, giving them her full attention.

"The Lilac Inn is haunted."

Chapter 15

"Lilac Inn is haunted," Morgan repeated.

"We've heard rumors about a ghost and figured maybe it was a marketing ploy, but not after last night."

Morgan briefly thought about Randi's insistence she'd heard noises and glimpsed something in the water while setting up camp down by the beach.

"I forgot and left my cell phone charger in the car. Leah and I went down to get it," she added. "On our way back to our room, we stopped by the kitchen to grab some bottled water from the fridge."

Leah picked up. "And that's when Mia and I heard the basement door rattling."

Morgan's brows knitted. "Like someone was trying to get into the house?"

"Maybe." Leah lowered her voice. "We tracked Grace down and told her what was going on. She followed us back inside. By then, we were totally freaked out."

Quinn made a choking sound. "What happened?"

"Nothing." Mia shivered involuntarily. "Grace went down there with a flashlight to check it out but couldn't find anyone."

"It's possible another guest sneaked into an area where they shouldn't have been. They locked themselves out and by the time you came back inside, someone had let them in," Morgan theorized.

"Nope. Grace checked with the other guests. It wasn't one of them."

"Maybe you expected something to happen after hearing the place was haunted and your mind was playing tricks on you," Quinn said.

"Someone was rattling the basement door," Leah insisted. "Do you have any rooms available?"

"I have two suites. One of them has double beds." Despite being thrilled at the idea of filling an empty suite, Morgan was reluctant to take the business at her friend's expense. "Does Grace know you're checking out early?"

"She offered us a refund and even suggested we check with you," Mia said. "We'll take the suite with double beds."

Morgan made quick work of checking the women in, all the while consumed by guilt about taking her friend's guests. She handed them the keys and texted Greg, who offered to meet them in the parking lot to grab their bags.

Quinn waited until they were gone. "Do you think Charlotte Coates' ghost was pounding on the basement door?"

"I thought ghosts typically floated through doors, not rattled them. I have no idea what happened, but as soon as they're settled in, I'm going to track Grace down."

The women returned and Morgan escorted them to the room, all the while going over everything they would need, rattling off the evening's social hour and the morning breakfast schedule.

"We noticed canoes and kayaks down by the beach and were thinking about taking them out," Mia said.

"You're free to use them. You'll need to sign them out, making note of the time you left. Life jackets are in the storage building and so are the paddles." Morgan accompanied them to the back door, reiterating the requirement to sign the equipment out.

Quinn waited for her friend to return. "I wouldn't mind going with you to hear what Grace has to say. Hopefully, the beach isn't haunted too."

"The beach." Morgan snapped her fingers. "Thanks for the reminder. Something else odd happened last night. I'll be right back." She ran upstairs and lightly knocked on Somewhere in Time's hallway door. The door opened and a bleary-eyed Randi appeared. "Good morning, Morgan."

"Good morning, Randi. Did you camp out on the beach all night?"

"Only for a few hours. The whooshing noise kept me awake. I finally packed everything up and came back to my room. Has anyone ever mentioned UFO sightings here on the island?"

"Not necessarily UFOs, but as Ronni and I mentioned last night, we have heard rumors about a woman who haunts the place next door." Morgan briefly told her about the sisters, the rattling basement door, and how they were freaked out. "I

164

suppose the fact we have a small cemetery nearby might play into their fears."

Randi perked up. "A cemetery?"

"I want to chat with Grace to find out if she has any idea about what may have happened." Morgan turned to go, and Randi stopped her. "I could use a leisurely stroll through an old cemetery to give my eyes a break from the computer."

Morgan wrinkled her nose. "I'm not sure my idea of a relaxing walk would be through a cemetery but to each his own."

The women trekked down the stairs to the front hall, where Quinn stood waiting. "Randi wants to wander around the cemetery. I'll show her how to get there on our way to Grace's place." Morgan sent a quick text and received a prompt reply.

"She's in the rear gardens and told us to meet her there." Morgan tucked her phone in her pocket and followed Quinn and Randi to the porch. The trio circled around the front, passing through her recently acquired parking lot.

The Coates family had been instrumental in helping Morgan get her B&B up and running. If not for them and their generous offer to sell a parcel of their property, enabling her to add the required parking lot, she wouldn't have a thriving business.

Which made her feel guilty all over again about Locke Pointe's new arrivals. Taking money right out of her close friend's pocket felt like a betrayal.

Quinn nudged her. "What's with the glum face?"

"I feel like a traitor, like the worst kind of lowlife for stealing Grace's guests."

"They checked out of the Lilac Inn," Quinn reminded her. "You happened to be next door and had rooms available. It's not your fault they left."

"True, but still..."

It took a few minutes for the trio to figure out how to find Grace's garden, which was tucked away in the back corner, behind a storage shed and adjacent to the island's small cemetery.

Morgan was the first to spot her kneeling on the ground. She caught her eye and gave a quick wave.

"Hey, Morgan." Grace pulled her gardening gloves off and dropped them in the wicker basket beside her.

"Good morning." Morgan briefly introduced Randi as Lynn Spade, her guest.

"It's nice to meet you." Grace changed the subject. "I had two guests check out this morning. I believe they were headed your way, looking for a place to stay."

"Leah and Mia. They showed up on my doorstep less than an hour ago. What happened last night?"

Grace filled them in, repeating the same story, about how the sisters had gone to their vehicle to get their cell phone charger. Upon returning, they stopped by the kitchen to grab some bottled water, and the basement door started rattling.

"Your basement door is in your kitchen?" Morgan asked. "I don't know if I've ever noticed it before."

"We call it a Michigan basement."

"A Michigan basement?" Quinn echoed.

"There are different variations. Mine was once a crawl space. It's not a pretty place. The floors are dirt and the ceilings are low."

"It sounds kinda creepy," Morgan said.

"It can be. I don't keep anything down there because it's damp." Grace placed her pruners in the basket. "If someone sneaked into my basement, they didn't find much."

"Do you think the sisters heard something?"

"I'm not sure. What I do know is they're convinced they had."

"It wasn't one of your other guests snooping around who accidentally got locked out?" Quinn asked.

"Nope. I checked with all of them, which is when Mia and Leah told me they weren't comfortable staying another night."

"So you refunded their money and suggested they check with me," Morgan said. "I appreciate you sending them my way, but I feel so guilty."

"Don't. I figured I might as well give you the business instead of sending them to the hotel over by the harbor."

"I camped out on the beach for a while last night," Randi said. "I'm almost positive I heard some strange noises and saw something floating over the water."

"Floating over the water?" Grace grimaced. "Like a ghost?"

"Looking back, it could have been lights from a small boat passing by. There was also an odd whooshing sound around the same time."

"I'm sure it was Ollie, our resident owl."

"Ollie the owl." Randi thought about it for a minute. "Yeah. It could've been."

"Maybe my great-grandmother has visited again," Grace said. "She drowned in Lake Huron."

"Does she rattle basement doors?" Randi asked.

"Not that I can ever remember." Grace slowly stood. "The other guests don't seem bothered by what Mia and Leah claim to have experienced. I hope it doesn't happen again."

Randi pivoted. "So where's this nifty old cemetery located?"

"I'll show you." Morgan motioned to Grace's gardening basket. "Let me walk Randi next door. I'll be right back."

A puzzled expression crossed Grace's face. It quickly faded. "Sure. Quinn and I will wait here."

Morgan walked her guest to the arbored entrance and returned to where Grace and Quinn stood waiting.

"Did you point your guest in the right direction?"

"I did."

"She likes cemeteries," Grace said.

"Yeah. It kind of fits in with her line of work."

"You called her Lynn *and* Randi."

Morgan could feel the blood drain from her face. Had she slipped? Apparently so. "I...uh..."

"She looks vaguely familiar, like the famous archaeologist, Randi Colbane. So, who is she...Lynn Spade or Randi Colbane?"

Chapter 16

"I'm...uh."

"Morgan Easton." Grace feigned a hurt look, placing a hand on her hip. "We're friends."

"We are."

"You can level with me. Is the woman I met Randi Colbane?"

"It is." Morgan hurried on. "She's the niece of my grandmother's close friend, Gerard Ainsworth. They came to the island together."

"She's also a famous archaeologist," Grace said. "I've been keeping up with the local news. A lot of islanders believe she's in the area searching for the Shifting Sands Medallion."

Morgan knew there was no way around it and leveled with her friend. "She's here because of the medallion."

"Cool beans. I hope she finds it." Grace started to pace. "Do you have any idea what this could do for business? The Lilac Inn will book up for years in advance if people think it's here."

"True, but it also means the island will be overrun with reporters, gold diggers, treasure hunters, and heaven only knows who else."

Grace abruptly stopped. "Good point. Her being here and looking for the medallion is definitely a double-edged sword."

Morgan didn't bother correcting her, pointing out that the medallion had already been found.

"No wonder she was excited about roaming around our cemetery. Hopefully, she doesn't start digging people up."

"I doubt she would," Morgan said. "She's slightly eccentric, but a good person. As far as her being here, I'm asking you—friend-to-friend—to keep it to yourself."

Grace placed a finger to her lips. "Your secret is safe with me."

"Thank you." Morgan changed the subject. "About the rattling doors."

"I think I know what happened last night. Follow me." Grace meandered along the side of the gardens, making her way to the inn's back door with Quinn and Morgan close behind.

Once inside the kitchen, she crossed over to the other side and adjusted the thermostat on the wall. Less than a minute later, the basement door rattled. "We recently replaced the main furnace and air-conditioning unit."

"The heat must have kicked on when they were in the kitchen. The force of air through the vents is making the door rattle," Morgan said. "Mystery solved. I'll let your former guests know we figured out what was rattling. Maybe they'll decide to check back in."

"It's too late," Grace said. "I've already booked someone to stay in the suite they vacated."

"Which means the inn is full," Quinn quipped.

Knock. Knock.

"I think I see your you-know-who guest standing on my stoop." Grace hurried off and returned with Randi by her side.

"I thought you might still be over here," she said. "The cemetery, although cozy and quaint, is small."

"The only people buried there are Easton Islanders," Grace said. "Can I offer you a lemonade or iced tea?"

"Thanks, but I'm good. I figured I would pop in to see if you pinpointed what was making the door rattle."

"A new furnace with powerful vents." Grace flitted across the room. "Are you sure I can't get you something to drink?"

"I appreciate the offer, but I have bottled water back in my room." Randi patted her head. "You're staring. What is it? Do I have a bug crawling on me?"

"N-no," Grace stammered. "I don't mean to stare. It's just...I can't believe a famous archaeologist is standing in my kitchen."

Randi shot Morgan a puzzled look. "You told her?"

"I slipped and called you Randi. Grace caught it."

"I won't tell anyone. Seriously." Grace clasped her hands. "Your job sounds fascinating. What has been your favorite find, if you don't mind me asking?"

"My favorite find?" Randi scratched the back of her neck. "It would be hard to pick one."

"How about the most disappointing one?" Quinn asked.

"Now, that would be easy." Randi shared a story about a dig in St. Augustine, Florida, the oldest city in the US. "A word of advice. If you ever visit the area and the Fountain of Youth, I suggest you take a pass on drinking the water."

"Because no one wants to live forever?"

"No. Because it tastes like sulfur." Randi glanced at her watch. "I would love to hang out and chitchat, but I need to get going. I have a few calls to make."

"I hope to see you again before you leave, Ms. Spade," Grace said. "Or whatever name you're using."

"Lynn Spade, at least for the time being," Randi said. "Despite the cemetery being a little lackluster, it was super interesting. This island is getting more intriguing by the minute. Spooky sounds, old cemeteries. I've officially added Easton Island to my list of semi-retirement possibilities. In fact, I'm putting it at the top."

Grace thanked her friends for stopping by to help solve the mystery and followed them to the front porch. "Good luck on your...project."

"Thanks. I'm pretty sure this one is almost in the bag."

While Quinn left to head home, Randi returned to Locke Pointe and Morgan meandered around the yard, regretting her slip of the lip and the fact Grace now knew who the woman was. She trusted her friend to keep quiet, but the circle of those "in the know" was growing, which meant the risk of someone else slipping was growing too.

She heard tires crunching on gravel and glimpsed a Locke Village patrol car pull up out front. Wyatt exited the driver's side and strolled across the lawn. "I was in the neighborhood, saw your SUV, and figured I would stop by. How's it going with Colbane?"

"She's keeping things interesting." Morgan briefly filled him in. "To sum her up, she's quirky, eccentric, and interesting."

"And also entertaining. At least she's working in style and comfort," he joked.

"Not always." Morgan reminded him how she and Ronni had found the woman setting up camp down by the beach.

"I'm sure she has some stories to tell."

"Including spending time in Kilimanjaro, jungles, deserts, near the Nile River."

Wyatt let out a low whistle. "It sounds exciting."

"And dangerous. We're still waiting for confirmation about the medallion's authenticity."

"How is she doing on researching who it might belong to?"

"She claims she's still working on it, although my gut tells me she already has a clear answer and just isn't sharing it with me yet."

Wyatt sneaked in a kiss. "Are you still up for a ride on my motorcycle or have you forgotten about our date with all that's been going on?"

Morgan placed a light hand on his chest. "No way. I could use a little fresh air to decompress."

"I have a special surprise."

"Are you taking me back to the waterfall?"

"You'll have to wait and see." Wyatt tapped his radio. "I gotta get going. I'll be by the house to pick you up later."

Morgan lingered in Locke Pointe's driveway, long after he left. From the moment Randi had arrived, it had been non-stop. The medallion, trying to keep her identity a secret, Grace's potential crisis, figuring out a way to help Greg.

Yet something told her life was smooth sailing compared to what it would be like in the very near future.

Chapter 17

"Where are you off to this evening?" Morgan sipped her ice water, eyeing Quinn, who waltzed into the kitchen wearing a little black dress with a crème-colored knit sweater over the top. She caught a whiff of her friend's favorite perfume. As she drew closer, Morgan noticed she was wearing mascara and lipstick, something she rarely bothered with.

"Out."

"Out where?" Morgan, her curiosity piqued, set her glass on the counter, giving her bestie her full attention.

"To a bar down by the harbor. A local from the mainland stopped by the gallery the other day and we got to talking. He told me he and his band were playing in Easton Harbor this weekend and invited me to come listen to them."

"I like live music."

"I would have invited you, but you already made plans with Wyatt," Quinn reminded her. "There's a small arts and crafts festival going on, so I might check it out while I'm there."

Morgan's cell phone chimed. It was Wyatt giving her a heads up that he would be there soon to pick her up.

"Gotta run." Quinn slipped out the back door before Morgan had a chance to ask her when she would be home, not that she was her friend's keeper, but for safety's sake, they made a point of knowing each other's schedules.

"C'mon, Chester. Let's check out the gardens while we wait for Wyatt."

The pup dashed down the steps and made a beeline for his favorite bush before tromping over to the gardens.

They carefully made their way up and down the rows, inspecting the fruits and vegetables. Chester stopped when he reached the fence separating their property from her neighbor, Mrs. Bixby's.

She caught a movement out of the corner of her eye. It was Mr. Pickles; her rabbit...the one Chester had rescued the previous winter.

Her pup squeezed under the fence and trotted over to greet him.

Morgan called him to come back, but it was too late. The rear door flew open and her neighbor slowly made her way down the steps.

"Come over here, Mr. Pickles." The rabbit ignored the woman as he and Chester began prancing back and forth, chasing one another.

"Here we go," Morgan whispered under her breath. She'd often spotted the older woman wheeling her trash to the road, but had never gotten close enough to get a good look at her, other than the time she returned the rabbit after Chester's rescue.

Much to Morgan's surprise, or more like shock, she approached the fence. "Hello...Morgan."

"Hello, Mrs. Bixby. Chester and Mr. Pickles are getting reacquainted."

"He loves to watch you and Chester out in the yard." She motioned to the side of her house. "The window is his favorite spot."

"Chester has never met a stranger."

"He's an inquisitive pup and intelligent."

"Very." Morgan laughed. "I swear he knows what I'm saying to him."

"I read in the paper you turned your grandparents' home into Locke Pointe Bed-and-Breakfast."

"I did."

"How is it going?"

Morgan tipped her hand back and forth. "It's a little slow. I'm not sold out like the Lilac Inn next door, but each day we're getting busier."

"I knew your grandparents, Ann and Joseph."

Morgan's heart skipped a beat. "You did?"

Her neighbor nodded. "They were some of the nicest people."

"I wish I could remember them, but I was so young when I left the island."

"And your mother." Mrs. Bixby gazed over Morgan's shoulder. "She was the sweetest woman. She spent a lot of time tending her garden. We would stand right here at the fence and chat like you and I are doing now."

"I suppose you would have known my father, too."

Their eyes met, and the woman looked away. "I knew him. He was a good-looking man, but not particularly friendly."

"I'm sorry if he was rude to you," Morgan apologized.

Mrs. Bixby reached out her worn, weathered hand and patted Morgan's. "There is no need for you to apologize for your father."

"Did they...did my mom seem happy?"

"Laura loved Looking Glass Cottage. It was everything to her. Of course, Ann and Joseph visited often." Her expression grew far away. "I still remember the day she brought you and your twin brother home from the hospital. You were the most adorable babies."

Morgan held her breath, waiting for more, for a deeper glimpse into her mother's life on Easton Island, living in her beloved cottage, during the happiest years of her married life. And some of the saddest.

"In the summer months, she took you out in your stroller for a walk each day. Of course, she would stop by so I could visit with you. She was so proud of you and such a wonderful mother."

"I never knew about my brother Rhett until after Mom's death."

A flicker of surprise crossed the woman's face. "I'm sorry to hear that, Morgan. His death was devastating to Laura. I suppose your father was heartbroken too. He wasn't around much near the end and..."

"The fighting started," Morgan guessed. "According to my grandmother, they had some terrible arguments. He even ended up being arrested."

Mrs. Bixby looked away. "I was the neighbor who called the police the night it happened."

Morgan blinked rapidly, trying to process what her neighbor had just said. Mrs. Bixby was the one who had overheard her parents arguing and called the police. "I knew a neighbor called the police. I didn't know it was you."

"Rhett never forgave me. In fact, he came by my house not long after it happened. I suppose it was right after he got out of jail. He told me if I ever stuck my nose in his family's business again, I would regret it."

"Mom left not long after."

Mrs. Bixby nodded. "I felt somewhat responsible for her leaving."

Morgan's mind whirled, the pieces falling into place about why her neighbor had been standoffish. She thought Morgan was upset with her for calling the police on her father.

"You did the right thing and may have saved Mom's life," she said softly. "Please don't carry that guilt around with you. I would never hold it against you."

Mrs. Bixby's lower lip quivered. "I was afraid... I thought Laura was mad at me."

"Mom would never be mad at you for protecting her from an abusive husband."

The woman reached into her apron pocket. She removed a faded photograph and held it out. "I took this picture of you and your brother. I've been meaning to bring it over and thought you might like to have it."

Morgan studied the photo of two infants in identical baby bouncers. It looked as if they were on a picnic table in the backyard. Something about the photo looked vaguely familiar. She squinted her eyes, studying the pink crocheted sweater she was wearing. "I recognize the sweater I'm wearing."

"I made it for you. One for you and one for your brother. You looked so darling in them."

"Mrs. Bixby..."

"Please, call me Beatrice."

"Beatrice. Can you wait here for one minute? I want to show you something."

"Sure."

Morgan ran into the house, to her bedroom closet, and tracked down a box on the corner shelf, one she hadn't opened in a very long time. She removed her baby book and carefully set it on the bed before digging through the small stack of infant clothes her mother had hung onto.

Finally, she found what she was looking for and returned to where the woman stood waiting. Morgan held up the sweater.

Mrs. Bixby's eyes widened. "You still have it."

"Mom kept this, along with a handful of other baby clothes. It was special to her."

Tears welled up in the elderly woman's eyes. "Can I see it?"

Morgan handed the sweater to her, watching as a range of emotions played out. "Mom never forgot about you, Beatrice. She hung onto the sweater because it was special and *you* made it for me."

"I felt so awful about what happened after that night. One minute Laura was here. The next, she was gone. I never got to tell her how sorry I was or say goodbye."

Morgan impulsively hugged her and could feel the woman's shoulders sag. "Mom wasn't angry. I'm sure she was grateful. Dad could have hurt her, hurt me."

"All of these years, I felt so guilty about butting in, but I was so afraid for her," she whispered.

"Please know Mom appreciated what you did, even if she never told you." Morgan held up the photo. "Thank you for the photo and the sweater. I'll treasure both forever."

"You're welcome, and thank you for not being angry at me." Mrs. Bixby called her bunny rabbit, who obediently hopped back across the yard. She scooped him up and carried him the rest of the way to the house.

"You are a sweet woman, Beatrice Bixby, and I am so sorry you carried the guilt of my father's actions around for all these years." Morgan carefully folded the infant sweater and carried that, along with the precious photo of her and her brother, back to the cottage.

Chapter 18

"He's here, Chester." Morgan flung the front door open and found Wyatt standing on her stoop, holding a bouquet of long-stemmed pink and red roses.

Her eyes lit. "Roses for me?"

"No. I brought them for Chester," Wyatt teased. "Of course they're for you, silly."

Morgan reached for the bouquet. "You're spoiling me rotten."

"That's the plan." Wyatt tenderly kissed her before patting Chester's head. "There's my buddy. Have you been staying out of trouble?"

"He's been a good boy. I promised him a long walk after we get back from our date."

"Change of plans. Chester can come with us."

"On your motorcycle? Is that even safe?" Morgan carried the roses into the kitchen.

"I have a surprise. Well, multiple surprises. The roses, something for Chester, and then one more I'll show you before dinner." Wyatt told her as soon as she finished arranging the flowers, he would show them his second surprise.

"Did you hear that, buddy? Wyatt has something for you."

Chester wiggled his way in between them, gazing up at one and then the other.

"He's wondering what it is." Wyatt laughed.

"Crazy dog." Morgan finished filling the vase with water and placed her flowers in the middle of the kitchen counter. She took a step back to admire her handiwork. "They're absolutely beautiful."

"Just like you." Wyatt stepped in behind her. He slipped both arms around Morgan's waist and held her close. "You smell exotic."

"Exotic?" Morgan shifted to the side to catch his eye. "In a good way, I hope."

"In an alluring and romantic way. Whatever it is, the perfume is my new favorite," Wyatt murmured.

"I'll have to stock up." Morgan wrapped her arms around his neck. "Thank you for the flowers and for planning special dates."

"You're welcome. I plan to make plans for many years to come." Wyatt reluctantly released his grip and nodded toward the door where Chester stood impatiently waiting. "I think someone wants to go outside and see his surprise."

As soon as the door opened, Chester scrambled down the steps. The couple caught up with him in front of Wyatt's motorcycle. Morgan immediately noticed something was different. "You added a sidecar."

"For Chester." Wyatt scooped the pup up and placed him inside.

With head down and nose activated, he promptly sniffed every square inch of the sidecar. Giving it the "Chester seal of approval," he promptly plopped down and placed his front paw on the frame.

"I think he likes it."

"That's not all." Wyatt opened the rear storage compartment, removed a blue leather cap, and slid it on the pup's head.

Morgan burst out laughing as Wyatt gently tugged Chester's ears through the openings. After finishing, he strapped on a pair of goggles and fastened them in the back.

Woof. Chester barked loudly, shaking his head from side to side.

"He hasn't decided if he likes the goggles," Wyatt said.

"Give him time. Something tells me he's going to love riding with us."

Wyatt showed her a special harness. It attached to the inside of the sidecar, securing the pup yet giving him enough freedom to curl up and rest or sit upright when he wanted to see out.

"It's awesome." Morgan clapped her hands. "We're ready to hit the road."

"Almost." Wyatt nudged her dressy shoes with the tip of his sneaker. "You're gonna want to change into something a little more outdoorsy."

"Outdoorsy? Are you taking me back to Whisper Brook Waterfall?"

"That's a good guess." Wyatt's expression grew mischievous. "Not this time."

"We're going hunting or fishing?"

"Nope."

"I give up."

"Grab a sweater and swap out those sexy flats for some sneakers. You might even need your sunglasses."

Morgan darted back inside, where she traded her favorite flats for socks and sneakers. She dug through her closet until finding a light jacket, one she sometimes wore for her evening walks, a pair of old sunglasses and some bug spray for good measure.

She shoved everything into her backpack and caught up with Wyatt and Chester at the end of the driveway. "I brought bug spray, too."

"We might need it." Wyatt tugged on the chin strap to make sure Chester's helmet and goggles were securely in place. "I think he's ready to ride." He handed Morgan her helmet and slipped his on. "I checked the weather before I left. We might get a sprinkle or two, so I figured we would embark on our mini adventure first and then eat later."

"Sounds good." Morgan swung her leg over the side of the bike and settled onto her seat with Chester watching, a look of pure joy on his furry face, or at least the part not covered by goggles.

Wyatt revved up the engine. He swung around in a wide circle and they were off, cruising along the coastline.

Morgan snuggled closer to her boyfriend, leaning her head against his broad back. She glanced down, smiling widely when she noticed Chester sitting upright, his ears flapping in the wind while his head bobbed from side to side, as if he couldn't take it all in fast enough.

Wyatt slowed when they reached Locke Village. He turned right, cruising along the main street. Morgan noticed Elin Jensen and Ariel Vanmeter standing outside the Bean Brewing coffee shop, chatting.

Wyatt tapped the horn, catching the women's attention, and they both waved.

Morgan waved back and then pointed at Chester, who was looking their way.

Taking the back streets, Wyatt passed by the building department and library before returning to the main road that circled the island.

It was an easy ride. Morgan could feel the stress and tension, worrying about the medallion and Grace's discovery about who Randi was, started to fade. Life was good on Easton Island. More than good. It was wonderful.

Wyatt slowed and veered to the right, cutting through the center of the island until reaching Easton Harbor.

"Quinn's in town." Wyatt pointed to their friend's car parked in front of the harbor's bar.

Morgan noticed her brother's car parked next to it. "Do we have time to make a quick stop and show Brett and Quinn Chester's sweet new ride?"

"Your wish is my command." Wyatt slowed and pulled into an empty parking spot.

"I won't be long." Morgan slid off the seat and jogged down the sidewalk.

Near the bar's entrance, she could hear loud music playing and slipped inside. It took a minute for her eyes to adjust to the dimly lit interior. There wasn't an empty seat to be found.

Morgan skirted the edge of the crowd until she finally glimpsed her friend and brother seated at a center table, along with several others, including a few people who looked vaguely familiar.

Brett was the first to notice her. "Hey, Morgan. What's up?"

"Wyatt and I are cruising around on his motorcycle. We saw your car parked out front and thought we would stop by to say hi and show you something."

"Outside?" Quinn asked.

"Yeah. It will only take a minute."

Brett set his drink on the table and nudged the man on his right. "Watch our drinks. We'll be back in a few."

The trio crossed to the exit and stepped onto the sidewalk, passing by a large group of people who were on their way in.

"Quinn wasn't kidding when she told me this band was popular," Morgan said.

"They're up and coming and have a strong following," Quinn said. "You and Wyatt should hang out with us for a while."

"We would, but Wyatt has other plans." Morgan pointed to her sneakers. "Something involving casual clothing and bug spray."

They reached Wyatt's motorcycle, and Quinn burst out laughing when she spotted Chester, who was still sitting in the sidecar, helmet and goggles, firmly in place.

"Chester looks like a miniature biker dude."

"Wyatt added the sidecar so he could ride with us."

Brett playfully flicked the pup's ear. "He looks like he's ready to roll."

"How's it going?" Wyatt shook Brett's hand.

"Can't complain. I haven't seen you around much lately."

"Which is a good thing if I'm in uniform," Wyatt joked.

"You said it. Maybe after you're done with the ride, you can swing back by for a drink."

"Thanks for the invite, but we'll have to take a raincheck," Wyatt said. "Morgan and I have some other stuff planned for this evening."

The couples chatted for a few more minutes, admiring Chester's sporty new look before the pup grew restless and began pawing Wyatt's arm.

"I think Chester is telling us it's time to hit the road again."

"It's a good look, buddy." Quinn snapped a picture of the pup. Wyatt and Morgan posed with him, and then they did a selfie, with all four of them and Chester front and center.

Wyatt finished taking the final photo with his cell phone and tapped the screen.

Morgan peered over his shoulder. "Who are you texting?"

"Grady MacDonald. He's meeting us."

"Now?"

"Yep."

"But..."

Wyatt pressed a finger to her lips. "Patience, grasshopper."

"Fine." Morgan slid her helmet back on.

"Have fun." Quinn and Brett waved as the couple sped off.

Instead of backtracking toward the center of the island, Wyatt turned right, heading along the shoreline. Across the street from Sunset Beach, where Morgan's grandfather had proposed to her grandmother, he turned onto a road which wasn't much more than a two-lane dirt track.

They jostled along at a slow speed until reaching a shiny Harley-Davidson parked off to the side. "Is that Grady's motorcycle?"

"Yeah. He bought it a couple months ago so we could ride together."

"It's nice. All he needs now is a girlfriend."

"That's what I keep telling him."

Morgan remembered Grace's comment some time ago about Grady being out of her league. "Grace is a sweetheart. I bet they would have fun together."

"Grace Coates?" Wyatt hung his helmet on the handlebar. "Don't tell me you're going to play matchmaker," he teased.

"I dunno." Morgan shrugged while mentally warming to the idea. "Maybe."

Chester hopped out of the sidecar, his attention laser-focused on a nearby bush.

Morgan stopped him before he could escape. "We need to take the goggles and helmet off first." She promptly removed both and placed them inside the storage bin.

Wyatt grasped her hand and began leading her into the forest. The flat path quickly turned into an uphill climb. They had almost reached the top when he abruptly stopped. "Close your eyes."

"Why?"

"To get ready for your surprise."

Morgan closed her eyes, trusting Wyatt to lead her the rest of the way. They must have reached a clearing because she could tell it was getting lighter and brighter.

"You can open them now."

Her eyes flew open. "What in the world?"

Chapter 19

Wyatt could barely contain his excitement as he dragged Morgan toward the wooden platform where Grady, whose expression matched his friend's, stood waiting.

"What is this?" Morgan studied the side of the post and a complicated series of straps. The straps looped at the top, crisscrossing metal cables which ran above the treetops for as far as the eye could see.

"It's a zip line," Wyatt said. "Grady and I built it."

"This thing is a blast." Grady proudly patted the harness gear. "Wyatt clocked me going thirty the other day."

"Thirty miles an hour?" Morgan wrinkled her nose. "Is it safe?"

"One hundred percent. We've been zipping along it for a couple weeks now, every chance we get."

"Other than me and Grady, you'll be the first to test it out," Wyatt said.

Morgan started to shake her head, but when she noticed the look in her boyfriend's eyes, so full of hope, his excitement and pride over what he and his friend had built, she didn't have the heart to tell him no. "I...suppose. Just once."

Wyatt whooped. "We'll have you strapped in and ready to go in no time."

The men worked together, securing Morgan in an array of loops and straps until she was certain there was no way she could untangle herself. "Where will I end up?"

"At the bottom of the hill." Grady pointed to a camo-colored four-wheeler parked nearby. "I'll drive down to the other platform. After you land, I'll unhook the gear and give you a ride back up here."

"You'll need this." Wyatt grabbed a helmet and helped Morgan put it on.

"You're positive I'm not going to crash to the ground?"

"No way. Even if the gear somehow disengages, the treetops will cushion your fall," Grady said.

"That makes me feel better," Morgan said sarcastically. "And how will you get me out of the trees?"

"You'll have to shimmy down to the ground." Wyatt flicked her chin. "Kidding. I'm kidding. You won't crash. I promise."

Morgan took a tentative step toward the edge of the platform. Visions of the harness and straps somehow coming off and her toppling into the treetops filled her head.

Chester, who had been circling the trio, pawed at her leg, a look of concern etched on his small face. "Chester is worried about me."

"He's excited for you," Grady corrected.

Wyatt lightly punched his friend's arm. "Hey, maybe we can rig up a harness system for Chester and…"

"No." Morgan made a slicing motion across her neck. "Chester is not zip-lining."

"Fair enough, although after your first zip, you might change your mind."

Morgan whispered a small prayer as she studied her surroundings. God had saved her life after Jason abducted her. Surely, he wasn't going to let her topple into the trees.

"Seriously, it's a blast," Wyatt promised. "You'll want to do it again."

"If you say so." Morgan sucked in a breath. She cautiously crept toward the edge of the platform and peered down the embankment. Something told her if there was any sort of mishap, it was going to hurt…a lot.

"Hold up." Grady hopped onto the ground. "I'll head down to the other end. Let me know when Morgan's ready to go."

Wyatt grabbed the walkie-talkie sitting on the small wooden stand. "Will do."

"See you in a few." Grady climbed on the four-wheeler and sped off.

Morgan began to feel lightheaded. *What have I gotten myself into?*

Wyatt loves you. There's no way he would put you in any danger.

Accidents happen.

Stop! She silently scolded herself.

"You're sure I'll be safe?"

"Absolutely." Wyatt began fiddling with her helmet.

"What are you doing?"

"Turning the recorder on so we can watch replays of the action."

"Replays of me screaming my head off?"

"If that's what you're going to do." Wyatt chuckled. "I'm not sure if I've ever heard you scream."

"You will today. Guaranteed." Morgan nervously tugged on the chin strap. "If I don't make it out of this alive, please make sure Chester's taken care of. Maybe you and Quinn can work out some sort of joint custody."

"You're not going to die." Wyatt's walkie-talkie crackled. It was Grady. "Hey, Wyatt. I'm here. Whenever you're ready, let her rip potato chip."

"You got it. Morgan is on her way just as soon as I can talk her off the platform." He set the walkie-talkie down. "Are you ready?"

"As ready as I'll ever be." Her heart began hammering in her chest when she felt her boyfriend's hands on her shoulders. Morgan braced herself and closed her eyes. "On the count of three."

"Sounds good." She sucked in a breath. "One...two..."

"Three!" Wyatt gave her a firm nudge and off she went. For a fraction of a second, her feet dangled beneath her and then *WHOOMP*. A whoosh of air blasted her in the face.

If you're going to crash, you might as well enjoy the ride. Morgan opened her eyes to the most amazing view...a canopy of pine trees. Beyond the trees was a meadow of lush green grass filled with a carpet of purple wildflowers.

She lifted her gaze, admiring patches of blue sky peeking out between pillows of thick fluffy clouds. Through a clearing, she glimpsed Lake Huron and Morgan began to feel like she was soaring...weightless.

Gripping the harness with her left hand, she flung her right hand out, flying across the skies as free as a bird. All too soon, she dipped down. She could see Grady up ahead, waiting for her.

Morgan slowed enough to land lightly on the platform.

"Well?" Grady asked. "How was it?"

"Incredible," Morgan said breathlessly. "It felt like I was flying over the treetops, soaring with the breeze."

"Would you do it again?"

"In a heartbeat. I can't wait to play the recording."

Grady worked quickly to help unstrap Morgan. After finishing, they hopped onto the four-wheeler and drove back up the hill where Chester and a beaming Wyatt waited. "What did you think?"

"The view is incredible. I was soaring over the trees." Morgan placed her hands on her cheeks. "It was the coolest thing ever."

"I take it that means you want to go again?"

"Yes, but not before you both get to zip." Morgan offered to drive to the ending point while Grady geared up.

The trio took turns with Morgan snapping action shots. She got a thumbs up from Wyatt on his way down and started to turn her phone off when it rang. It was Quinn.

"Hey, Quinn."

"Hey, Morgan. I forgot my house key and locked myself out."

"Bummer. You're already home? I figured you would be out late tonight."

"Change of plans."

Morgan could tell by the tone of her friend's voice something had happened. She could also tell Quinn wasn't in the mood to discuss it. "I'm with Grady and Wyatt. Why don't you head on over and hang out with us for a while?"

"I'm kind of in a crappy mood," Quinn grumbled.

"I have something guaranteed to turn your frown upside down." Morgan told her friend how to find them. "Wyatt's and Grady's motorcycles are parked near the road."

"I don't want to spoil your date."

"Grady is here," Morgan reminded her. "There's no chance you'll spoil a romantic evening."

"Are you sure?"

"Positive."

"Okay. I'm on my way." Quinn started to hang up and Morgan stopped her. "You'll need some comfortable shoes."

"I have an extra pair of gardening shoes in my trunk, along with some sweatpants and an old t-shirt."

"That'll work. I guess it pays to have a trunk full of junk," Morgan teased.

"You know it."

Grady waited for Morgan to end the call. "Quinn's coming by?"

"Yeah. She got locked out of the house. I'll wait for her out by the road."

Wyatt made a move to go with her, and Morgan stopped him, suspecting she might want a few moments alone with her friend to find out what was going on. "You two hang out here. Chester and I will meet Quinn."

"Are you sure?" Wyatt asked.

"Positive."

"Holler if you need us," Grady said. "We're only a minute away."

"Will do." Morgan, with her pup by her side, took the trail back, passing by the motorcycles on her way. Chester spotted his sidecar. He ran over and hopped in, clearly ready for another ride.

"Not yet, goofy." Morgan scooped him up and set him on the ground. "We need to wait for Quinn."

217

Her friend's car crested the hill. Morgan flagged her down and waited for her to park. "That was fast."

"There wasn't much else to do, considering I'm locked out of the house." She slammed the driver's side door and shoved her keys in her pocket. "Where are Grady and Wyatt?"

"In the woods."

Quinn frowned. "Wyatt took you on a date with Grady?"

"No. I mean. Well...I guess he did... sort of. It's fun."

"I'm not feeling very fun."

"What happened? It looked like you and Brett were having a good time hanging out earlier."

"We were until Felicia came along," Quinn said glumly.

"Who is Felicia?"

"His ex-girlfriend."

"I've never heard him mention her name. What does that have to do with you leaving?"

"Because she was flirting with him and he didn't seem to mind. I didn't feel like watching them together." Quinn lowered her gaze. "If he's interested, I figured it was in my best interest to vamoose."

"What makes you think they were flirting?"

"Oh, Brett." Quinn pressed her hands to her chest and batted her eyes. "I forgot how awesome of a pool player you were. I'm all elbows. Can you show me a few of your tricks?"

Morgan burst out laughing. "Show me a few of your tricks? She said that?"

"Something along those lines. I felt like a third wheel, so I told him I was getting a headache and left."

"But you don't have a headache."

"Not yet," Quinn said. "Although if I had hung around much longer watching them, I would have developed a migraine."

Morgan flung her arm around her bestie as they meandered down the path. "I wouldn't worry about it. If Brett's attracted to her and they're flirting, maybe he's open to rekindling their romance."

"More power to them," Quinn grimaced. "Where are you taking me? These woods remind me of a scary movie scene involving chainsaws and ramshackle red barns with torture tools lining the walls."

"Have I ever told you that you have a very vivid imagination?" Morgan nudged her friend forward. "What you're about to do will make you forget all about flirty Felicia."

"Are you sure?"

"Positive."

Chapter 20

Quinn landed lightly on the platform and let out a loud shriek. Grady, who was waiting at the bottom, easily caught her and helped her unhook the harness. "Morgan wasn't kidding about how rad the ride was."

"It's a whole new level of excitement," he said. "Morgan and Wyatt invited me to head over to the harbor to have dinner. The clouds finally cleared, which means Harbor Dockside's outdoor patio is going to have an amazing sunset view."

"I am kinda hungry." Quinn patted her stomach. "Isn't the restaurant right next door to the bar?"

"We shouldn't have any trouble getting a table. Everyone is over listening to the band while we'll be quietly enjoying our meal."

"It sounds tempting, but I hate to be a date crasher."

"We'll both be date crashers," Grady pointed out. "If Wyatt and Morgan didn't want company, they wouldn't have invited me."

"True."

The couple caught up with Wyatt and Morgan, who were packing up the zip lining gear.

"I invited Quinn to head down to the harbor with us for dinner."

Morgan eased the harness into the storage bag and handed it to Wyatt. "Your headache never materialized?"

"Nope."

"Then join us for a bite to eat."

"I don't want to be a fourth wheel."

"You'll never be a fourth wheel. Something tells me the sunset is going to be spectacular. Let's enjoy it while we can."

Quinn reminded them she had her car and promised to meet them there. She left first, followed by Grady.

Morgan and Wyatt were the last to leave, spending extra time making sure Chester was properly geared up and ready for the ride.

Arriving at the restaurant, the group caught up near the entrance and snagged a corner table near the water, offering an unobstructed view of the harbor. Faint strains of the band echoed along the alley, but not so loud that the group couldn't talk.

"I'm starving." Morgan perused the menu. "Chicken tenders with ranch dressing sounds good."

"I was thinking the same thing."

Grady elbowed Quinn who was sitting on his right. "Dinner is my treat. You said you were hungry. How about we start with an order of mozzarella sticks?"

"You don't have to..."

He cut her off. "It's settled. I'm buying your dinner."

Morgan sipped the fruity drink she'd ordered. "We should do this more often."

"Agreed." Grady lifted his glass. "Here's to good friends and great adventures."

"Friends and adventures," Wyatt echoed, lifting his glass. "There's nothing better."

While they ate, the friends took turns throwing out ideas about adding to the zipline, creating another section that would take the thrill-seekers even deeper into the woods.

"We would have to do some heavy-duty tree trimming," Wyatt warned. "I'm not sure we have the right equipment."

"At least not this year." Grady slipped Chester, who was making his rounds under the table, a piece of hamburger.

The pup gobbled up the tasty treat and licked Grady's hand to show his appreciation.

"No wonder Chester won't sit still," Morgan laughed. "He's feasting like a king."

Quinn leaned back in her chair. "Tonight was one of the best nights I've had in a long time. Thanks for inviting me."

"You're welcome," Wyatt said. "Grady and I couldn't wait to show off the zip line."

Morgan snuggled closer and planted a kiss on Wyatt's cheek. "It was a blast. We'll have to do it again."

"We have the entire summer to enjoy the outdoors."

"I wonder if Grace Coates would like to check out our zip line," Grady said.

Quinn caught Morgan's eye and winked. "I'm sure she would. Why don't you ask her?"

"I..." Grady's cheeks turned a tinge of pink. "She's always so busy running the inn."

"True, but everyone needs a day off," Morgan said softly. "I can almost guarantee Grace would jump at the chance to try it."

"It wouldn't be like a date or anything." Grady started stumbling over his words. "We can...I mean, others can come along too."

"What's wrong with asking Grace out on a date?" Wyatt asked. "She's single. You're single."

"I'll add my two cents and agree with Quinn and Wyatt," Morgan said. "In fact, I'm so certain she'll accept your invitation that, if she doesn't, you can eat breakfast at my B&B for free for the next month," she bargained.

"You can't lose either way." Wyatt chuckled. "Free breakfast or a date with one of the cutest gals on the island."

"True."

The group lingered until the sun finished setting. With the bills paid, the friends strolled back to their vehicles.

"Can I borrow your house key?" Quinn asked.

"Sure." Morgan tossed her the keys. "Don't head to bed and lock me out."

"I have an early shift," Wyatt said. "I'll be bringing Chester and Morgan home before too long."

The pup, who was investigating a potted plant, circled back around.

"Why don't I take Chester home with me?"

Morgan scratched his ears. "Do you want to go home with Quinn?"

Woof.

"I think Chester is saying yes." Quinn tapped Grady's arm. "Thank you for dinner. You and Wyatt did a great job of making sure we didn't crash and burn."

Grady shoved his hands in his pocket. "I'm glad you didn't have to sit home."

"Or sit in my car waiting for Morgan." Quinn clicked her key fob and eased the driver's side door open. She waited for Chester to scramble across the seat before climbing in. "Thanks again."

Quinn drove off while the trio trekked toward their motorcycles which were parked nearby.

The bar's front door opened, and Brett, who was with several others, appeared. He said something to one of them and strolled down the sidewalk. "Hey Morgan, Wyatt." He shook Grady's hand. "Officer MacDonald."

"Mr. Easton," Grady replied.

"Did I just see Quinn drive off?"

"She forgot her house keys and tracked me down to borrow mine."

Grady, unaware of the earlier incident and Quinn making an excuse to leave the bar because of

Brett's ex, spoke up. "We convinced her to come zip lining with us and grabbed a bite to eat afterwards."

Brett's eyes narrowed. "Quinn went zip lining? I thought she had a headache."

"I...she felt better," Morgan blurted out. "After leaving here, she drove home and realized she locked her house keys inside. She called me to see if she could borrow mine and I talked her into going zip lining with us."

Judging by the expression on Brett's face, his sister knew he wasn't buying it.

"Seriously. It's the truth." Morgan nodded toward the group Brett had exited the bar with, noting the fact that none of them was a female. "How was the band?"

"Better than I thought they would be."

"We could use more live music around here." Wyatt reached for Morgan's hand. "Maybe one day you can check out our zip line."

"Count me in."

The group made small talk until Brett's friends called him back over.

Grady waited until he was gone. "What just happened? Have I created a little conflict between Quinn and your brother? Because it sure seemed like it."

"Brett's ex showed up at the bar and started flirting with him. Quinn wasn't in the mood to hang around and left after complaining that she was getting a headache."

Grady arched a brow. "And I opened my big mouth and told him we spent the last couple of hours zip lining and having dinner."

"It wasn't your fault. You had no idea. Love can be a complicated thing." Morgan sighed. "Especially when neither person is ready to admit they're interested."

"Tell Quinn I'm sorry if I threw her under the bus." Grady parted ways with them, claiming he needed to stop by the police station. Meanwhile, Morgan and Wyatt hopped on the motorcycle for the cruise back home.

Reaching the cottage, Wyatt climbed off first before giving Morgan a hand. He pulled her into his arms and tenderly kissed her lips. "Thank you for being such a good sport about date night."

"It was fun." Morgan ran a light hand across his cheek, her heart pitter-pattering when she caught a whiff of his cologne mingled with the earthy scent of being outdoors. "I have to say one thing...you sure know how to keep me on my toes."

"And your feet off the ground," he joked.

"I wouldn't have it any other way." She flung both arms around his neck, feeling his warmth through his open jacket. Morgan closed her eyes, savoring the moment. All the emotions of being in love filled her.

Wyatt was everything she could ever hope for...thoughtful, caring, protective, generous, handsome. And he loved Chester.

Finally, reluctantly, he climbed back on his motorcycle and waited for Morgan to reach the porch. She blew him a kiss. Playing along, he caught it with his hand before backing out of the driveway and disappearing into the night.

Morgan could see the living room light was on. She sucked in a breath and gave the front door a light knock, since she no longer had a house key. She was not looking forward to telling her best friend they may have inadvertently caused major conflict as far as Brett was concerned.

Chapter 21

"You're sure you aren't upset?" Morgan followed her friend into the kitchen.

"Nope. Not one iota. It's not like Brett and I are seeing each other," Quinn said. "He has his life. I have mine. I was feeling the onset of a migraine. It went away, so I hung out with you guys. End of story."

"At least you have a heads-up in case he mentions it to you." Despite warning her best friend the previous night, and Quinn seeming not at all concerned, Morgan *had* worried about it. The last thing she wanted to do was cause conflict.

Although it hadn't been Morgan who had potentially created an issue so there was no reason to feel guilty. She'd given her friend her blessing if she was interested in pursuing a relationship with her brother.

On the flip side, Morgan had not had a conversation with Brett to give her blessing. Perhaps that was where the disconnect was happening. Her brother wasn't sure how his sister would react.

Regardless, the ball was in Brett's court. If he wanted to open the line of communication, it was all on him. To be honest, it was none of her business, or at least *mostly* none of her business, other than caring about her close friend and brother.

"I spoke to Randi already this morning. She told me she should have the authentication confirmation sometime today."

"Cool," Quinn said. "And then you'll find out who it belongs to."

"Yeah. She seems confident about tracing its origins, although something tells me it could get complicated."

"Whenever money is involved or a piece of history is on the line, it's almost a given."

Morgan consulted her watch. "I need to run over to Locke Pointe before noon for a meeting with Ronni."

Quinn slid off the stool. "And I'm on my way to the art gallery. Keep me posted on Randi's findings. This could be the discovery of the decade."

Morgan promised she would. After her friend left, she wandered aimlessly through the cottage, drawn to the fireplace mantle and the photograph of Morgan and her mother. It was next to a more recent photo of her and Elizabeth, seated inside a rare sports car belonging to the estate, right before she and her grandmother embarked on a memory-making cruise around the island.

It reminded her about Gerard's visit and what Randi had said, how the man loved Elizabeth and was hoping they might rekindle their romance. Perhaps the timing was off before, but maybe now both were open to reigniting their relationship.

Was Elizabeth ill and keeping it a secret from her grandchildren? She'd been adamant about not wanting to discuss recent changes in the Easton household and the specialist Ben had referred to. Which caused Morgan even greater concern.

And even though the terrifying thought something was wrong lingered in the back of her mind, Morgan knew her grandmother well enough to know she wasn't going to "spill the beans" if there were any "beans to spill" until she was good and ready.

It didn't take long for Morgan to shower, throw on some old shorts and a T-shirt, and head out. She pulled into her new parking lot, only a stone's throw from the Lilac Inn, and noticed an Easton Harbor patrol car parked in the driveway.

Morgan exited her vehicle and circled around, tiptoeing along the thick hedge that separated their properties and could hear the tinkle of Grace's laughter along with Grady's deep voice. She peeked through the bushes and glimpsed the two of them sitting on the porch swing.

"Way to go, Grady," she whispered. "You didn't waste any time." Thrilled to think another romance might be blossoming, there was a spring in her step as she strolled back across the parking lot to Locke Pointe.

She made her way into the dining room and found breakfast was in full swing. Morgan greeted her guests, lingering when she reached Mia and Leah's table. "How was your first night's stay in the Lilac Twin suite?"

"Wonderful," Leah said. "We slept like babies. It was so peaceful."

"I'm glad to hear it. No ghostly sightings or strange bumps in the night?" Morgan asked.

"No."

"I spoke with Grace at length about what happened to you. We believe what you may have heard was the furnace turning on. The pressure of air forced through the vents rattled the basement door."

Mia's eyes widened. She nudged her sister. "I told you it wasn't a ghost."

"You were as freaked out as I was."

"As much as I enjoy having you stay here at Locke Pointe, Grace is my friend, and I wanted to set the record straight in case you ever decide to visit Easton Island again."

"We plan to." Leah nodded enthusiastically. "We were just talking about riding bikes into town today. Mia and I sampled the coffee you left in our basket of treats, along with those delicious aebelskivers. We want to stock up on goodies to take home."

"Bean Brewing and Danish Delight Bakery are both great little shops." Morgan reminded them to sign the bikes out before making her way into the kitchen.

She found Tina bustling back and forth. "Good morning, Morgan."

"Good morning. Can I give you a hand?"

"Sure." The cook handed her a bowl of cookie dough. "I'm whipping up a batch of cherry chocolate chunk cookies using Traverse City area cherries."

"Traverse City," Morgan repeated. "The name sounds familiar. Is it in Michigan?"

"It sure is." Tina held her hand up, palm side toward her. "It's over here, on this side of the state."

Morgan grinned. "I love how Michiganders point out locations using their hands."

"Michigan is the Mitten State. I guess I don't even think about it anymore."

"It's pretty cool. Not everyone can use their hand to show people where they live. In fact, I'm going to start using my Michigan mitten hand to show others where Easton Island is located." Morgan slipped an apron on and began placing heaping teaspoons of dough on the greased cookie sheets before sliding them into the oven.

"Something smells divine." Ronni breezed into the kitchen and peeked in the oven. "Are those my cherry chocolate chunk cookies?"

"You betcha." Tina beamed. "Thanks for the recipe. They'll be a tasty treat for the guests later this afternoon. I like to make cookies that are anything but cutter."

"You're welcome." Ronni's cell phone chimed. "I need to head to the office." She caught Morgan's eye. "Are we still on for our morning meeting?"

"Yes. I'll catch up with you." After finishing, she made her way into the office, where she discovered Ronni was still on her phone.

"I'll be a few minutes," she whispered.

"No problem." Morgan motioned that she was going outside and slipped out through the back door. She caught up with Greg near the storage shed and found him rearranging the life jackets. "Hey, Morgan. I was just gonna track you down."

"What's up?"

"I want to show you something." Greg led her down the hill to the beach and the spot where Randi had previously pitched her tent. "There are some weird holes in the ground, like someone has been digging around."

"The holes are from tent stakes."

Greg scratched his head. "Tent stakes?"

"Lynn Spade, one of our guests, set up camp here the other night. She was having trouble sleeping."

"Strange." His brows furrowed. "I mean, not your guest, but why bother paying for a fancy suite when you're gonna sleep outside?"

Morgan patted his arm. "Let's just say she has some unusual habits and quirks. I appreciate you bringing it to my attention."

"You're welcome."

She turned to go, and Greg stopped her. "I also wanted to thank you again."

"For what?"

"Everything." Greg kicked at the hole, avoiding her gaze. It was something Morgan discovered he did when he was nervous. "I've always kind of struggled to find a job I could stick with."

Morgan's tone softened. "You like working at Locke Pointe?"

His head shot up. "Yes, ma'am. I love it. Being outdoors, helping people, and working at my own pace."

"Not everyone can handle high-pressure jobs."

"Which is me. Captain Davey tried to help, but I couldn't keep up at the docks. I know he felt bad about letting me go."

"And there isn't enough work to keep you busy helping your uncle at Easton Estate."

"I've always been a misfit, a little slow at keeping up. I never found my place until now."

Morgan's throat clogged at his confession, how he stood before her, swallowing his pride and expressing his gratitude. "You're doing a great job, a wonderful job, Greg. The guests always compliment you. They tell me how you make them feel welcome from the moment they arrive, how you take the time to share your love for Easton Island."

His eyes lit. "They do?"

She nodded. "You're Locke Pointe's ambassador, and I couldn't be prouder of you."

Greg shoved his hands in his pockets. "That means a lot to me, Morgan. You're like an angel God brought here to help people like me."

It was Morgan's turn to become emotional, and she gave him a quick hug. "I guess we're both kind of misfits and have finally found our place, huh?"

"We did. Yes, ma'am, we sure did."

Chapter 22

By mid-afternoon, Morgan was a bundle of nerves, seesawing back and forth between believing the reason Randi hadn't heard back about the medallion was because her colleague was having trouble confirming the authenticity and believing he had already done so and was broadcasting it to the archaeological world.

Colbane was keeping a low profile, which may have been an understatement, considering she stayed locked up in her room for most of the day, only coming down once to get some fresh air and take a long walk along the shoreline.

Morgan kept an eye out for her return and caught up with her as she started up the stairs. "Hello, Lynn. How's it going? Any word yet?"

"No, but I should be hearing something soon." Lynn tapped the top of her watch, reminding Morgan that California was three hours behind. "It's only noon there."

"Good point. It's just that I've been..." She ran a hand through her hair. "Stressed out."

"I understand, and I'll let you know the second I hear from Newt."

"Thank you." Morgan tracked down her pup and they headed out. Their first stop was the flower gardens, which were flourishing under Greg's care.

Chester made a beeline for the hill and was halfway down before Morgan could catch up. The wind suddenly picked up, creating small swells on the open water while storm clouds gathered overhead.

"We can't go too far, buddy," Morgan warned her pup. "It looks like it's going to storm."

Droplets of rain started to fall, and they picked up the pace, hurrying back to their private beach area. She checked to make sure the storage shed and water toys were secure before scrambling up the hill and to the house.

As soon as they reached the front porch, the skies opened and rain poured down. Big, beautiful droplets soaked the grass and watered her flowers.

The rest of the afternoon slipped by while Morgan distracted herself by updating the reservation schedule and answering emails. The evening's social hour arrived, and she joined her guests, noting everyone was there except for Lynn / Randi.

Ronni, who had returned from running errands, joined them and pulled Morgan aside. "We're under a thunderstorm watch."

"We should let the guests know in case they have evening outdoor plans. You start on this side of the room. I'll handle the other." She and Ronni split up, each stopping to give their guests a heads up about the potentially severe weather.

Morgan helped gather the empty dishes and carried them out of the parlor, nearly colliding with Lynn, who was barreling down the hall. "Hey, Morgan."

"Hello, Lynn. We missed you during our social hour."

"I've been busy working on my...research."

Morgan tightened her grip on the dishes, an inkling of concern creeping up her back. "Is everything all right?"

"I have my colleague's opinion."

Morgan began to feel lightheaded. This was it...a confirmation which could easily turn her world upside down—again. "I would like my grandmother and Brett to be present."

"I understand. Assembling all interested parties might not be a bad idea," Randi said.

Morgan had forgotten Ronni was also collecting dirty dishes until she spoke. "What is going on? Is there some sort of issue involving Locke Pointe?"

"In a roundabout way. You might want to hang around." Morgan's hand trembled as she reached for her phone. She tapped out a group text to her grandmother, Brett, Quinn, and Wyatt.

Emergency meeting at Locke Pointe at 6:45.

Elizabeth was the first to reply. *We have a second opinion?*

Yes. Ronni is already here.

The others promptly replied they were on the way.

"I could sure use a nice, hot bath right about now." Randi placed a light hand on the back of her neck. "I've been hunched over my computer almost all day."

"The main suite is still unoccupied. Feel free to take a nice, long bath after our meeting."

"I'll be happy to give it a go."

Things moved fast as the family and friends assembled, all showing up separately except for Elizabeth and Gerard, who arrived together.

Quinn was last. "I hope I'm not late. I was waiting on a customer."

"No worries. Let's get this show on the road." Morgan directed them to the office and ran upstairs to grab Randi, who had returned to her room.

Morgan waited for her to step inside and closed the door behind them.

Elizabeth began counting heads. "It appears we're all here."

"I don't..." Ronni's voice trailed off. "I'm completely confused."

"You won't be for very long," Morgan said.

"We've been on pins and needles all day." Gerard motioned to his niece. "You have the confirmed findings?"

"I do." Randi reached into her pocket and pulled out a small white envelope. "The report is in here."

Morgan's heart hammered in her chest as she stared at the envelope. "Ronni, this isn't Lynn Spade. Her name is Randi Colbane. She's a world-renowned Biblical archaeologist who is here to authenticate the *Shifting Sands Medallion*. I found it hidden upstairs."

"I knew something was going on. I spotted the fake blond wig from a mile away," Ronni said. "How did you find the medallion?"

Morgan briefly filled her in, explaining how the star key had helped uncover the clues.

"That's incredible. It's been here the whole time."

"It has." Morgan could feel her armpits grow damp. "The authentication. What does...what does your colleague have to say?"

"You'll have to open it to find out. This is my favorite part of my job, presenting the results." Randi held the envelope out. "This is where the rubber meets the road. It's your baby. You do the honors."

Chapter 23

Morgan's hand shook as she took the envelope from Randi Colbane, the Biblical archaeologist, and knew whatever was inside could very well change her life forever.

She pressed it to her chest, her mind whirling. She wanted more than anything to have had a hand in tracking down one of the world's greatest treasures. Her grandparents had ensured the medallion remained safe, putting a great deal of thought into hiding it in a most interesting and unusual manner, tucked away for decades until Morgan found it. She would never forget that moment for as long as she lived.

On the flip side, the discovery could turn Easton Island from a quaint, cozy, and charming island into the most popular place on the planet, affecting the lives of islanders and residents for years to come.

"Well?" Quinn nudged her. "Are you going to open it?"

Morgan's eyes met her grandmother's. "This could change everything for everyone, including you."

"I understand the implications," Elizabeth said softly. "What are the other options?"

"Unfortunately, as soon as I uploaded the information to my colleague, the cat was out of the bag," Randi said.

"There's no turning back," Brett chimed in. "From the moment you and Wyatt found the box."

Morgan's jaw tightened as she ran her fingernail under the seal. She flipped the flap, removed the single sheet of paper, and unfolded it. Although most of the words were mumbo jumbo, a series of technical terms, there was one sentence she completely understood. "This is a verification of authenticity."

Quinn let out a loud whoop. "Girl, you are about to put Easton Island on the map!"

Morgan stood dazed while the others in the room congratulated each other on the extraordinary find. Randi and Gerard were thick in the mix, and everyone began talking at once.

Elizabeth slipped in next to her granddaughter. "Congratulations, my dear. Your mother and grandparents would be so proud. You have accomplished what they could not and, I might add, single-handedly."

"Not single-handedly." Morgan shook her head. "I had your help, along with Wyatt's help. Ronni was with me when I found the star-shaped key. It was a joint effort." She sensed someone standing behind her and turned to find Randi watching her. "Congrats, you lucky dog."

"I would say the same. Congratulations to you," Morgan said. "Our next step is to notify the rightful owners."

Randi motioned them over to the side of the desk. "My professional opinion, and based on the extensive research I've done, is it belongs to the Israeli people. I have the IAA—the Israel Antiquities Authority, along with the chief scientist's contact information. We've worked on a few projects together. I even took the liberty of drafting a letter for your approval. Once the letter is sent, we can coordinate the meeting for the artifact to change hands."

"I would like to do this as soon as possible," Morgan said. "Knowing it's authentic and having it in my possession is going to keep me up at night, even more so than now."

"Considering the artifact's history, I'm sure they'll move expeditiously to claim it from you," Randi said. "In other words, you won't have long to worry about it."

Elizabeth held a finger to her lips. "Regardless, as you pointed out...the cat is out of the bag. My suggestion is to get ahead of it."

"By holding some sort of news conference and announcing it before it leaks out," Morgan said. "Prissy is out of the question. She'll probably start a rumor, telling people I somehow stole it. I might have someone else in mind to cover the story."

"The young man from Florida who is a regular visitor to Easton Island," Elizabeth guessed.

"Spencer Veltman." Morgan motioned to Randi. "If I can get Spencer up here, would you be willing to come back for an interview?"

"Sure, as long as you let me stay at Locke Pointe," Randi bargained.

"It's a deal. Let me call him."

"Speaking of calls," Elizabeth said. "This calls for a celebration. While you track down the reporter, I brought a few bottles of Roederer Cristal Brut in the event a celebration was in order."

It took a few minutes for Morgan to locate Veltman's contact information. She dialed his number, scrambling to figure out what she would say when she left a message.

Much to her surprise, he picked up. "Morgan Easton."

"Hello, Spencer Veltman. I was expecting to leave a message."

"I have your number programmed in my phone, thinking maybe one day I would hear from you. Are you ready to give me an interview?"

"Actually, the reason I'm calling is that a big story is going to break soon, and I wondered if you might like to come up here to cover it. I think it could be very beneficial to your career."

There was a long silence on the other end of the line. So long that Morgan thought they had been disconnected. "Are you still there?"

"I'm here. When?"

"The sooner the better."

Rustling ensued on the other end. "I can arrange for some paid time off. It might take a day or two to confirm."

"Perfect. Please keep this to yourself," Morgan said. "Especially if you want credit for covering the breaking news story."

"You said this is big," Veltman said.

"You have no idea."

"I'll text my flight and itinerary as soon as I have it. In fact, I might be able to pull a few strings and be there even sooner."

"Thanks. I look forward to hearing from you." After ending the call, Morgan quietly tiptoed out of the room and down the hall to the living room.

She made her way over to the portrait near the piano, the one of her grandparents. Next to it was a more casual photo of Laura standing alongside her parents. It was one Morgan had recently framed after finding it in the album, hidden alongside the medallion.

All three were smiling, the sun shining brightly and nothing but clear skies behind them. A chill ran down Morgan's back and she could feel their presence so strongly, as if they were in the room standing next to her.

"I'm returning the medallion to the rightful owners. Can you believe it? After all these years of being hidden away, it's finally going home."

Morgan rubbed the goosebumps on her arm, her mother's presence merely a breath away. "The medallion is just like me, Mom. I finally found my way home."

The end.

The Series Continues!

Easton Island: Easton Family Dynasty
Coming Soon!

Dear Reader,

I hope you enjoyed reading, "Easton Island - A Most Unusual Guest." Would you please take a moment to leave a review? It would mean so much. Thank you! -Hope

Read More by Hope

Easton Island Mystery Series

Easton Island is the continuing saga of one woman's journey from incredible loss to finding a past she knew nothing about, including a family who both embraces and fears her and a charming island that draws her in. This inspirational women's fiction series is for lovers of family sagas, friendship, mysteries, and clean romance.

Cruise Director Millie Mystery Series

Cruise Director Millie Mystery Series is the new spin-off series from the wildly popular Millie's Cruise Ship Cozy Mysteries.

Millie's Cruise Ship Cozy Mystery Series

Hoping for a fresh start after her recent divorce, sixty something Millie Sanders, lands her dream job as the assistant cruise director onboard the "Siren of the Seas." Too bad no one told her murder is on the itinerary.

Lack of Luxury Series (Liz and the Garden Girls)

Green Acres meets the Golden Girls in this brand new cozy mystery spin-off series featuring Liz and the Garden Girls!

Made in Savannah Cozy Mystery Series

After the mysterious death of her mafia "made man" husband, Carlita Garlucci makes a shocking discovery. Follow the Garlucci family saga as Carlita and her daughter try to escape their NY mob ties and make a fresh start in Savannah, Georgia. They soon realize you can run but can't hide from your past.

Garden Girls Cozy Mystery Series

A lonely widow finds new purpose for her life when she and her senior friends help solve a murder in their small Midwestern town.

Garden Girls - The Golden Years

The brand new spin-off series of the Garden Girls Mystery series! You'll enjoy the same fun-loving characters as they solve mysteries in the cozy town of Belhaven. Each book will focus on one of the Garden Girls as they enter their "golden years."

Divine Cozy Mystery Series

After relocating to the tiny town of Divine, Kansas, strange and mysterious things begin to happen to businesswoman, Jo Pepperdine and those around her.

Samantha Rite Mystery Series

Heartbroken after her recent divorce, a single mother is persuaded to book a cruise and soon finds herself caught in the middle of a deadly adventure. Will she make it out alive?

Sweet Southern Sleuths Short Stories Series

Twin sisters with completely opposite personalities become amateur sleuths when a dead body is discovered in their recently inherited home in Misery, Mississippi.

Join The Fun

Get Updates On New Releases, FREE and Discounted eBooks, Giveaways, & More!

<u>hopecallaghan.com</u>

Meet Hope Callaghan

Hope Callaghan is an American mystery author who loves to write clean, fun-filled women's fiction mysteries with a touch of faith and romance. She is the author of more than 100 novels in ten different series.

Born and raised in a small town in West Michigan, she now lives in Florida with her husband. She is the proud mother of 3 wonderful children.

When she's not doing the thing she loves best - writing mysteries - she enjoys cooking, traveling and reading books.

Get a free cozy mystery book, new release alerts, and giveaways at hopecallaghan.com

Bonus - Recipe

Canadian Prairies Flapper Pie

<u>Ingredients</u>:

Crust:
½ cup butter or margarine
1 ¼ cups graham cracker crumbs
¼ cup granulated sugar

Filling:
2 1/2 cups of milk
1/2 cup of white sugar
1/4 cup of cornstarch
3 egg yolks
1 tsp vanilla
1/8 pinch of salt

Meringue Topping:

3 egg whites, room temperature

1/4 cup of sugar

1/4 tsp of cream of tartar

Directions:

Preheat oven to 350 degrees.

-In large saucepan, blend all filling ingredients.

- Cook on a medium heat until it boils.

-Stir constantly until it thickens.

-Turn burner off.

-Set aside to cool while you make the meringue.

-In a small bowl and using a hand mixer, beat the meringue ingredients on high until forming stiff peaks.

-Set aside.

-Lightly spray the inside a 9" pie tin with cooking spray.

-Mix pie crust ingredients together.

-Press evenly against bottom and sides of the pie tin.

-Pour the filling into the crust.

-Top with the meringue, swirling lightly to create little spikes.

-Place pie into preheated oven.

-Bake until the meringue browns, around 10 minutes. Check prior to ten minutes to ensure the meringue doesn't overbake.

-After cooling, place in fridge.

-Serve promptly.

Made in the USA
Monee, IL
10 November 2024

69770405R00163